KAYA AND THE RIVER GIRL

KAYA · 1764

BY JANET SHAW

ILLUSTRATIONS BILL FARNSWORTH

VIGNETTES RENÉE GRAEF, SUSAN MCALILEY

THE AMERICAN GIRLS COLLECTION®

Published by Pleasant Company Publications
For information, address: Book Editor, Pleasant Company Publications,
8400 Fairway Place, P.O. Box 620998, Middleton, WI 53562.

Visit our Web site at **americangirl.com**

Printed in Singapore.
03 04 05 06 07 08 09 10 TWP 10 9 8 7 6 5 4 3 2

Library of Congress Cataloging-in-Publication Data

Shaw, Janet Beeler, 1937–
Kaya and the river girl / by Janet Shaw ;
illustrations, Bill Farnsworth ; vignettes, Renée Graef, Susan McAliley.
p. cm. — (The American girls collection)
Summary: Kaya becomes jealous of a girl from another tribe until
they are forced to work together in a dangerous situation. Includes
historical notes on Indian trading along the Columbia River in 1764,
as well as instructions for creating a petroglyph.
ISBN 1-58485-792-7
[1. Jealousy—Fiction. 2. Nez Perce Indians—Fiction.
3. Indians of North America—Northwest, Pacific—Fiction.
4. Northwest, Pacific—History—18th century—Fiction.]
I. Farnsworth, Bill, ill. II. Graef, Renée, ill.
III. McAliley, Susan, ill. IV. Title. V. Series.
PZ7.S53423 Kawf 2003
[Fic]—dc21   2002031274

The
AMERICAN GIRLS
COLLECTION®

PICTURE CREDITS
The following individuals and organizations have generously given permission to
reprint illustrations contained in "Looking Back":
p. 32—Oregon Historical Society (OrHi 89622); p. 33—photo by Wilma Roberts;
p. 34—Wishram basket, courtesy of the Burke Museum of Natural History and
Culture, catalog number 2-4250, basketry round bag, possibly Wasco;
p. 35—© CORBIS; p. 36—MSCUA, University of Washington Libraries (NA1972);
p. 37—© Pat O'Hara/CORBIS; p. 38—Idaho State Historical Society, photo by
E. Jane Gray (63.221-178); p. 39—Lewiston Tribune, ID;
p. 40, Photography by Jamie Young.

TABLE OF CONTENTS

TOE-TA
*Kaya's father, an
expert horseman and
wise village leader.*

EETSA
*Kaya's mother, who is a
good provider for her
family and village.*

KAYA
*An adventurous girl
with a generous spirit.*

BROWN DEER
*Kaya's sister, who is old
enough to court.*

SPEAKING RAIN
A blind girl who lives with Kaya's family and is a sister to her.

SPOTTED OWL
A river girl who befriends Speaking Rain

WING FEATHER AND SPARROW
Kaya's mischievous twin brothers.

Kaya and her family are *Nimíipuu*, known today as Nez Perce Indians. They speak the Nez Perce language, so you'll see some Nez Perce words in this book. "Kaya" is short for the Nez Perce name *Kaya'aton'my'*, which means "she who arranges rocks." You'll find the meanings of these and other Nez Perce words in the glossary on page 48.

KAYA AND THE RIVER GIRL

Kaya sat with her sister Speaking Rain on a plateau above the Big River. Tatlo lay beside Kaya, his pink tongue lolling. Speaking Rain was blind and couldn't play running games, but Kaya and the other girls had just finished a game of Shinny. Even though a strong wind blew up the river gorge, the summer evening was warm, and Kaya was hot and tired. As she rested, she worked on her toy horse. The little horse had legs of willow

sticks, a body of deerskin
stuffed with buffalo hair, and
a twist of buffalo hair for a tail.
Speaking Rain had twined hemp
cord to tie on the small saddle that Kaya
had fashioned from bent willow twigs.
The sisters loved working together.

"I'm coming to talk to you, *Nimíipuu*
girl!" a girl shouted to Kaya across the
playing field. "I want to ask you something!"

"Who's calling to you?" Speaking
Rain asked. "I don't recognize her voice."

Kaya looked up curiously at the girl
running toward her. "She's one of the
River People who live on the north shore,"
Kaya said. "We beat her and her friends

2

at Shinny. I don't know her name."

The girl halted beside Kaya and dropped to her knees. She had a pretty, round face with full lips and flashing eyes. A glowing copper bead was strung on the hemp cord she wore around her neck. "I'm Spotted Owl," she said, reaching out to stroke Kaya's toy horse. "I don't know your name, but I know you're a fast runner."

"*Katsee-yow-yow,*" Kaya said. She felt her warm face grow warmer at the compliment. "I'm Kaya. My sister is Speaking Rain. How did you learn to speak our language so well?"

"My mother's a trading partner with a Nimíipuu woman. I've often traveled upstream with my mother to trade with

*"I'm Spotted Owl," she said, reaching out
to stroke Kaya's toy horse.*

her partner, or she's come downstream to us, especially now during salmon fishing season." Spotted Owl jumped to her feet again. "I came to find you because I want us to race! Will you run against me?"

Speaking Rain clasped Kaya's arm. "Go on, race her, Kaya!"

Tatlo's tail thumped against Kaya's leg as if he were urging her to race, too.

Kaya loved to run races, and she often won, even against the boys. She'd seen that Spotted Owl was a fast runner in Shinny—it would be a good test to run against her. *Aa-heh*, let's race," Kaya said. "Our friends can set out the markers."

Quickly the girls gathered again on the playing field. They laid several white stones across the center of the field. From that centerline they walked a hundred paces toward each end of the field, where they placed other stones to mark starting points. "I'll be the starter," Little Fawn cried. "Take your places!"

Spotted Owl took her place at one end of the field. Kaya gave her pup to Speaking Rain, then stood at the opposite end of the field, facing her opponent. Little Fawn raised her hand. When she brought it down, both girls took off to see who could cross the centerline first.

Kaya's heart was beating hard and fast as she raced down the field. Spotted Owl was coming swiftly, her arms pumping, but Kaya felt so much strength in her legs that she knew she'd cross the finish line first. She was shocked to see Spotted Owl plunge across the line before she could reach it.

Kaya halted herself in a few steps and bent over, dragging in gasps of air. She heard the girls congratulating Spotted Owl. Just then, Tatlo bounded up and began licking Kaya's flaming face with his rough tongue. He seemed to be telling her that it didn't matter that she'd lost the race. But losing hurt her pride.

"Good race!" Spotted Owl called to her. "Let's have another one soon!"

Kaya knew she should praise Spotted Owl, but all Kaya could murmur

was "Aa-heh." She stayed bent over, gazing at the ground, until the others had left. Then she went dejectedly to sit with Speaking Rain.

"I wish you'd won, but I like that girl," Speaking Rain said. "She has a strong spirit, don't you think?"

Kaya didn't answer. Her sister's

8

words only added to her injured pride. She vowed to become stronger, to practice racing every time she went for water or wood or to help with the horses. She vowed that the next time she and Spotted Owl raced, she would win.

When Speaking Rain went across the river to stay with White Braids, her Salish mother, for a little while, Kaya missed her sister badly. After a few sleeps, Kaya crossed the river to meet Speaking Rain. Working to get stronger, Kaya ran all the way upstream to where the Salish camped. She found Speaking Rain sitting in the shade of a tepee. At her side sat Spotted Owl. They were playing with their dolls.

"Tawts may-we!" Spotted Owl greeted

Kaya as she came close.

Kaya was taken aback to find the girl she thought of as her rival playing with her sister, but she didn't want to let her bruised feelings show. "Tawts may-we," she said politely to Spotted Owl. "Tawts may-we, Sister!" she said much more warmly to Speaking Rain.

"Spotted Owl comes to see me every day!" Speaking Rain said. "She just asked if I'd like to go with her to her village to visit She Who Watches, the old chief who looks after her people. I'd like to go, wouldn't you?"

Kaya saw that Speaking Rain wore Spotted Owl's necklace with the copper bead. "That's a pretty necklace,"

Kaya said quietly.

"Aa-heh, Spotted Owl gave it to me," Speaking Rain said.

Spotted Owl smiled up at Kaya in her easy, open way. "Kaya, won't you come with us? It's very good to visit She Who Watches. The spirits are very strong at the place where she guards over my people."

"Come with us," Speaking Rain urged.

Kaya wouldn't refuse her sister's request, but she wished she could just grasp Speaking Rain's hand and lead her away from Spotted Owl. Kaya had only just been reunited with her sister, and Speaking Rain spent part of her time with White Braids, who had saved her life. Kaya knew it was selfish, but she didn't

want to share what little time she and
Speaking Rain had with this river girl.

Spotted Owl didn't seem to notice
Kaya's chilly silence as they walked
downstream. She was busy telling
the story of She Who Watches.

"A long time ago, in the time
before memories, my people had
a woman chief," Spotted Owl began.

"A woman?" Speaking Rain asked.
"Nimíipuu have many women leaders,
but our chiefs are always men."

"Our chiefs are men, too, now. But
this was long ago," Spotted Owl continued.
"Our chief was wise and kind and firm,
and my people revered her. Then
one day Coyote disguised himself in a

12

bearskin and came up the river to our village. He wanted to find out if my people were grateful for all he'd taught them and the gifts he'd given them.

"Coyote walked through the village beside our chief. He saw that the people had built warm lodges and had plenty to eat. They were rich with goods that others had traded to them for the salmon they'd caught. All seemed well, but our chief felt a shiver of fear. She guessed that the creature in the bearskin was Coyote and that he might try to trick her.

"When Coyote asked if she treated her people well, she kept her voice steady to show her courage. 'You've seen all that my people and I have accomplished together,' she said. 'You've seen that my people respect me. Most important of all, I teach my people to do good.'

"Coyote leaned forward, and the bearskin slipped off his head. 'Listen to me!' he growled. 'You've done well for your people, but the world on the river is going to change. New people will come, bringing great sickness and death. You will no longer be chief. Indeed, there will be no more women chiefs for your people.'

"'I will stay here as long as my people want me to lead them!' our chief said firmly.

"'Then it will be as you wish,' Coyote growled. 'Your time has come to an end, but nothing will separate you from your

14

people. Your name shall be She Who Watches, and you'll guard your people for all the years to come. This will be so!' Then Coyote slipped away, and no one has seen him since.

"When people went looking for our chief, she had vanished. They found instead a strange new face chipped into a pillar of rock—it was She Who Watches. And she's still guarding us after all these years," Spotted Owl said, finishing her story.

After a time the girls reached the place where She Who Watches looked out over the River People's village and across the wide river beyond. Kaya drew in a sharp breath when she looked up into the face of the old chief, still reminding her people to do good and live well.

"What do you see, Kaya?" Speaking Rain asked. "Tell me."

Kaya led her sister forward until they stood beneath the face etched into the reddish-gray basalt. "She's up there, higher than the tallest tepee pole," Kaya said. Then she stretched Speaking Rain's arms wide. "Her face is broader than your outstretched arms. Her eyes are huge and wide. She sees everything."

Speaking Rain raised her face toward the painted image above them. "Her eyes are made of stone, but she's not blind like me," she said softly.

"She sees with her heart, just as you do," Spotted Owl said kindly to Speaking Rain.

*Kaya drew in a sharp breath when she looked up into the face
of the old chief.*

17

"My sister is the kindest person that I know!" Kaya exclaimed. She wanted to be the one to praise her sister, not this river girl. After all, Kaya knew Speaking Rain better than anyone else did.

Spotted Owl didn't seem to notice Kaya's cold tone of voice. "Come have a meal with us," she said. "My mother's going to cook a big salmon that my father caught this morning. It will be delicious!"

"Katsee-yow-yow!" Speaking Rain said with pleasure.

"Katsee-yow-yow," Kaya echoed in a grim voice that hardly seemed her own. *Why can't I feel the way my sister does about this good-natured girl?* she asked herself.

18

Kaya looked up again at the wide, wise eyes of She Who Watches. Could the old chief show her some way to get rid of these painful feelings that she knew were wrong?

✿

But Kaya's bad feelings about Spotted Owl didn't disappear. When Speaking Rain praised her new friend, Kaya kept quiet. When her sister said she hoped Spotted Owl would come back and race again, Kaya bit her lip. She hoped she wouldn't have to think about Spotted Owl once the salmon runs were over and Kaya's band left the Big River.

One evening several canoes of River People crossed to the south side of the river for trading and games. A group of girls gathered at the playing field for a game of Shinny. Before the game began, Spotted Owl ran to greet Speaking Rain. But when Spotted Owl called a greeting to Kaya, Kaya pretended not to hear.

The river girls played hard and well, scoring two goals right away. Kaya tried even harder to help her team get ahead. The running she'd done had made her legs stronger, and she took the ball as often as she could, hoping to score a goal.

Kaya was racing with the ball out ahead of the others when Spotted Owl caught up with her. With a swift jab of her stick, Spotted Owl scooped the ball away from Kaya. "No you don't!" Kaya cried.

As she hurled herself after her opponent, Kaya shoved her stick between Spotted Owl's feet to try to get the ball back. Spotted Owl tripped on the stick, and Kaya bumped into her, pushing her to the ground and knocking the air out of her. Spotted Owl's teammates helped her off the field so she could catch her breath.

Alarmed that she'd hurt Spotted Owl in anger, Kaya went miserably to sit with Speaking Rain. For a time the girls sat in silence as Kaya struggled with her shame. "It's my fault Spotted Owl got hurt," Kaya finally admitted. "I've had bad feelings about her. Everything she does and says is good, yet I feel as if she's my enemy!"

Speaking Rain put her hand on Kaya's

21

shoulder. "Listen to me," she said gently. "It's true that Spotted Owl's a good person. In what she says and does, she's so much like you, Sister! You're both leaders. You're both strong. But we mustn't be like coyotes, who live alone. Our grandmother always tells us that we must be like wolves—strong individually, but always working together. She Who Watches must have taught that to her people, too."

Kaya rested her chin on her knees as she considered her sister's wise words. Slowly her churning feelings smoothed and she knew what she had to do. "I have to go after Spotted Owl," she murmured as she got to her feet.

Kaya put a horsehair rope on the chestnut mare that was staked near the tepees. Then she rode upstream to where the River People had beached their canoes. Some traders were already loading their canoes for the return crossing. Kaya scanned the crowd for Spotted Owl, but she wasn't there. Kaya rode farther upstream.

Around the bend, Kaya saw a strong-looking elder woman seated in the stern of her heavily loaded canoe. Spotted Owl was pushing out Elder Woman's canoe so that she could cross back to the other side.

Kaya dismounted and walked up the

shore toward Spotted Owl. As Kaya wondered what she could say to make things right, she watched Elder Woman's progress.

Elder Woman expertly guided the big canoe into the swift current. She pointed its bow upstream into the current so that she could ferry the canoe sideways to the opposite shore. But when the canoe was gliding by a rocky outcropping, her paddle struck underwater rocks. In an instant the paddle was snapped from her grip. Elder Woman leaned out, trying to grab her paddle. Kaya gasped when the force of the current tilted the canoe, tossing Elder Woman into the water.

Elder Woman was washed against the

outcropping. She tried to scramble up and away from the heavy canoe bearing down on her, pushed by the mighty river. Kaya watched in horror as the canoe plowed against Elder Woman's leg, smashing her against the rocks. Elder Woman cried out.

The powerful current dragged the canoe around the end of the outcropping and swept it downstream. Elder Woman clung to the outcropping, but she seemed to be in so much pain that Kaya worried she might pass out and be carried away by the rushing river.

Both Kaya and Spotted Owl knew that they had to work fast to rescue Elder Woman. The girls ran to another, smaller canoe nearby. They shoved the canoe into

the water, climbing in as it moved away
from shore. In the stern, Spotted Owl
angled the bow slightly upstream, and
they swept sideways out to where Elder
Woman was stranded. Kaya could see
Elder Woman's arms trembling as she
struggled to hold on to the rocks.

Spotted Owl guided the canoe into
the calm water on the downstream side of
the outcropping, where she held the canoe
still. *I must be strong!* Kaya thought as she
climbed swiftly from the prow onto the
rocks toward Elder Woman. Just before
Kaya could reach her, Elder Woman lost
her grip on the slippery rocks and began
to go under. Kaya lunged, seized the
woman under her arms, and pulled with

all her might, tearing Elder Woman from the churning waters. Kaya half-dragged and half-carried her across the rocks to the canoe. Elder Woman cried out again as Kaya eased her over the side and jumped in after her. Spotted Owl ferried back to shore, where other women had gathered.

"Take my horse!" Kaya cried as the

women lifted Elder Woman from the canoe. Quickly, they lashed a travois to the horse and helped Elder Woman onto it. They led the horse downstream to get aid for Elder Woman's injured leg.

Kaya's heart was thudding and her arms aching from the effort of the rescue. Spotted Owl's face was red and sweat ran into her eyes. But when their gazes met, they both smiled. "We worked well together," Spotted Owl said.

"Aa-heh, we did," Kaya agreed.

The girls splashed cold river water onto their faces. As Kaya wiped her eyes, a good thought came to her. "I want you to have my toy horse."

"I like that horse!" Spotted Owl said. "I'll trade you my doll for it."

"That's a fine trade," Kaya agreed. "Listen to me. You and I could be trading partners. Would you like that?"

When Spotted Owl nodded happily, Kaya took a deep breath. She felt as if she'd been underwater for a long, long time and now, at last, she could lift her head into the air again. She couldn't wait to tell Speaking Rain all that had happened and how she and Spotted Owl had worked together and become friends—for Kaya was certain that this was what She Who Watches must have wanted.

JANET SHAW

At 8   Now

When I was growing up in Missouri, I went to a camp at the Lake of the Ozarks to learn swimming and canoeing. Like Kaya, I thought I was strong and capable. But when a storm caught us in the middle of the lake, two friends made me sit in the middle of our canoe while they paddled us to safety. I was glad they were stronger than I!

Janet Shaw is the author of the Kirsten and Kaya books in The American Girls Collection.

Looking
Back
1764

A PEEK INTO
THE PAST

This late nineteenth-century photo shows the massive falls at Celilo.

In Kaya's time, tens of thousands of people from all over the Northwest gathered each summer to trade, fish, and socialize along the Columbia River at Celilo Falls. Some came from as far away as modern-day Montana, while others traveled east from the Pacific Ocean.

Spotted Owl's people, the Wishram, did not have to travel far at all. They were one of several tribes who set up permanent villages along the river.

Each tribe brought a different item to trade. Kaya's people traveled throughout the year, and they brought roasted camas roots from the high meadows. Spotted Owl's people lived along the river year round and offered dried salmon and salmon eggs to tribes who lived too far away from the river to fish.

Fresh salmon was smoked over a low fire.

Nez Perce baskets (left) were decorated with triangles, diamonds, and other geometric shapes to represent trees, mountains, and other landmarks in nature. Wishram baskets (right) also featured human and animal figures.

Baskets were common trade items for all tribes from the plateau region, including the Nez Perce and the Wishram. Baskets were used for gathering, storing, and preparing food. Tightly woven baskets could even be used to carry water.

Girls like Kaya and Spotted Owl began to learn how to weave when they were only about six years old. A girl's first basket, whether it was good or bad, was always given to an older, accomplished basket maker in her village or tribe. This was done out of respect and to help bring the girl luck in her future as a basket maker.

The Wishram were widely known for their unique round or flat twined bags made from dried beargrass and hemp. Women and girls used dried berries and plants to make dyes to color the materials they used to make their baskets.

Women also dried berries for food and for trade.

Many of the designs that were woven into baskets were also seen in ancient rock art on the bluffs above the Columbia River. No one knows for sure who made these early artworks, but the artists used their art to record what happened in their world, their beliefs, and their legends.

Rock art is commonly found in places, like Celilo Falls, where people gathered to trade and fish. These designs may have been created to mark a specific location

or as a special symbol, such as to show appreciation for the many fish that gave themselves for food.

Besides trading and fishing, the summer gathering at the Falls gave Kaya's and Spotted Owl's families a chance to see old friends and make new ones. Since every tribe spoke a different language, communicating was sometimes a challenge. Many people used sign language— a language

Rock art designs ranged from simple wavy lines to detailed images, including animals, hunters, and mythical beings, like She Who Watches.

of hand symbols that people from most tribes could understand.

Those who had a trading partner in another tribe often learned the language of their trading partner. Spotted Owl spoke Kaya's language because her mother had a Nez Perce trading partner and had learned to talk with her.

Trading partners exchanged gifts every time they saw each other. Each summer at Celilo Falls, and at other times throughout the

Young girls traded with girls their age from other tribes.

38

year, the partners traded woven bags or baskets, food, or maybe toys or clothing. Trading partners always knew they were welcome in the other's tribe. They often hunted or fished in each other's area, and sometimes they even arranged marriage between their children!

Trading partners were truly friends for life. Kaya and Spotted Owl's trade of the toy horse and doll might have been the first of many exchanges between the two friends.

Nez Perce girls today still learn traditional basket making.

An
American
Girls
Pastime

MAKE A PETROGLYPH
Tell a story in stone!

Kaya's and Spotted Owl's ancestors were rock artists. They made *petroglyphs* by scratching or chipping designs into a rock surface with a sharp stone. They made *pictographs* by painting images directly onto rocks with a bone or frayed stick paintbrush. Sometimes they used both methods on the same piece.

Use your creativity and some modern-day materials to create and decorate your own Native American petroglyph.

YOU WILL NEED:

An adult to help you

*1 cup powder craft plaster**

½ cup warm water

Container for mixing plaster

Spoon

Mold (small paper plate or Styrofoam bowl)

Plastic drinking straw (optional)

Carving tool (a skewer or screwdriver)

Acrylic paint

Paintbrush

Matte Mod Podge

Dark-colored cream shoe polish

Piece of rawhide (optional)

*Such as Faster Plaster, available at craft stores

1. Cover your work area with newspaper.
Wear old clothes.

Step 2   Step 3

2. Measure the plaster into the container
and add the water. Stir the mixture
with the spoon until it is smooth.

3. Pour the plaster mixture into the mold.
Gently tap the edge of the mold to bring
any air bubbles in the plaster to the
surface. Throw away extra plaster mixture and wash the bowl and spoon. Do
not pour down the drain.

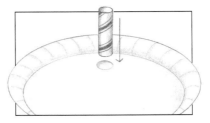

4. To make a hole to hang your petroglyph, place a piece of drinking straw near the top shortly after you pour the plaster.

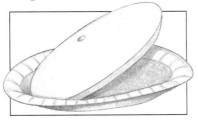

5. Let the plaster dry for 1 to 1½ hours, then remove the straw and peel away the mold. The plaster should be hardened but still feel slightly damp.

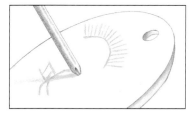

6. Use your carving tool to scratch a design into the plaster. The deeper you carve, the more the design will show up after you paint it. Let the petroglyph dry overnight.

7. Paint the petroglyph with acrylic paint or color it with shoe polish. After the paint is dry, brush the petroglyph with Mod Podge. Let dry.

8. To highlight your carvings, rub shoe polish over the images. Wipe away excess polish.

9. To hang, thread a piece of rawhide through the hole and tie with a knot.

Carve these designs into your rock or make up your own!

Rising Sun

Sun

Moon

Star

She Who Watches

Birds

People

Mountain Sheep

Turtle

River

Fish

GLOSSARY OF NEZ PERCE WORDS

In the story, Nez Perce words are spelled so that English readers can pronounce them. After each word below, you'll also see how the word is spelled by the Nez Perce people, how they pronounce the word, and what it means.

aa-heh/'éehe *(AA-heh)*—yes, that's right

katsee-yow-yow/qe'ci'yew'yew' *(KAHT-see-yow-yow)*— thank you

Kaya'aton'my' *('ky-YAAH-a-ton-my)*—she who arranges rocks

Nimíipuu *(nee-MEE-poo)*—The People; known today as the Nez Perce

tawts may-we/ta'c méeywi *(TAWTS MAY-wee)*—good morning

"*Maggie?*" Dillon called in concern. "*Are you okay?*"

She looked at him, one hand shielding her face as the giggles refused to go away.

He realized she was laughing and offered his hand to help her stand. Maggie started to slide again when her other shoe found the same slippery substance on the floor.

"Here, sit down," he said, holding on to her as he slid a chair behind her. He used several paper napkins to wipe the cake icing from the soles of her shoes. When he kneeled to slip them back onto her feet, the camera flashed again.

"Well, does the slipper fit?" Kim teased as she joined them.

"Perfectly," Dillon declared with a bow in the direction of the videographer.

"I got it all on tape," the man said happily.

TERRY FOWLER is a native Tar Heel who loves calling coastal North Carolina home. Single, she works full-time and is active in her small church. Her greatest pleasure comes in the way God has used her writing to share His message. Her hobbies include gardening, crafts, and genealogical research. Terry invites everyone to visit her Web page at terryfowler.net.

Books by Terry Fowler

HEARTSONG PRESENTS

HP298—A Sense of Belonging
HP346—Double Take
HP470—Carolina Pride
HP537—Close Enough to Perfect
HP629—Look to the Heart
HP722—Christmas Mommy
HP750—Except for Grace

Coming Home

Terry Fowler

Heartsong Presents

To those foster parents who find room in their hearts to provide homes to the children who need them.

And as always, special thanks to Mary and Tammy for taking the time to help me out.

Many thanks to the others who provided answers to my research questions.

A note from the Author:
I love to hear from my readers! You may correspond with me by writing:

Terry Fowler
Author Relations
PO Box 721
Uhrichsville, OH 44683

ISBN 978-1-59789-940-6

COMING HOME

All scripture quotations are taken from the King James Version of the Bible.

All of the characters and events in this book are fictitious. Any resemblance to actual persons, living or dead, or to actual events is purely coincidental.

Our mission is to publish and distribute inspirational products offering exceptional value and biblical encouragement to the masses.

PRINTED IN THE U.S.A.

one

"Okay, single ladies, we need you up front," Maggie Gregory announced to the reception party. "Kim's going to throw the bouquet."

Replacing the microphone in the stand, she scuttled off to the side with the furtiveness of a sand crab trying to avoid the incoming tide of women excited over the possibility of becoming the next bride.

"You, too, Maggie," Kim called when she spotted her friend's escape attempt. "There's no ring on that finger."

"Get over here," another girlfriend called from the center of the group.

Catching the throwaway version of the ribbon-bound bundle of red roses had never been a consideration for Maggie. Sure, she was a single attendant, but she was fifty years old. And she certainly didn't have a prince waiting to sweep her up into his arms and take her away from it all.

She moved around the outer fringes to the back of the group. When Kim turned for her toss, Maggie took a step back toward the crowd. Her high-heeled shoe slipped on the tile floor.

Feeling herself falling, Maggie struggled to regain her balance. A little scream left her lips when she failed.

Things moved in a blur of slow motion. She felt hands at her back as she tumbled backward, taking her would-be rescuer down with her into an ignominious heap on the fellowship hall floor.

"Are you okay?"

She glanced up as the pastor's four-year-old's big eyes widened and he yelled, "Look, Mommy, Miss Maggie knocked Mr. Dillon down."

Maggie wanted to disappear as all eyes turned their way. "I'm fine. You?"

The bouquet chose that moment to bounce off the ceiling fan right into Maggie's arms, and the photographer recorded the scene for posterity.

"What a waste," Maggie Gregory muttered, grimacing at Kim when she walked over to where they sat on the floor.

"What happened?"

"I slipped on something. Everything's okay. Go toss your garter or something."

"You're next," Kim confirmed with a big smile.

"Cornerstone's going to have more than one old maid if they wait for me to get married," Maggie guaranteed, turning her head to look straight into Dillon Rogers's blue eyes.

Neither paid any attention when the single women moved aside for the men. Dillon extricated himself, and when he tried to stand, the sole of his leather dress shoe slipped on her satin dress. They both heard the ominous rip at the same time. "I'm sorry, Maggie."

Things couldn't get any worse. "Never mind."

The laughter started when the garter hit Dillon's chest. They both looked at Wyatt, who innocently held up his hands, and the camera flashed again.

Maggie felt her face flame with embarrassment. "I'm glad everyone finds this funny."

"Sometimes you just gotta laugh with them," Dillon said.

She wiggled her bare foot, checking to make sure she hadn't injured her ankle, and glanced around. "Do you see my shoe anywhere?"

Dillon scouted for the clear shoe, looking under the long cloths that draped the tables with no luck. Finally, he spotted it hanging out of a large handbag. "There it is," he said, indicating their predicament. "Do you know her?"

Maggie shrugged and shook her head, watching as Dillon tapped the guest on the shoulder. "Excuse me, ma'am, could I possibly trouble you for that shoe in your purse?"

The woman looked at him as if he'd lost his mind but pulled her bag out from under the table. Her surprise registered. She used two fingers to pass him the shoe before she grabbed a napkin and cleaned her hand. "You need to wipe the icing off the sole before it throws her down again."

He smiled. "We will. Thanks."

The humor of the moment struck, and Maggie covered her face with her hands as the laughter started.

"Maggie?" Dillon called in concern. "Are you okay?"

She looked at him, one hand shielding her face as the giggles refused to go away.

He realized she was laughing and offered his hand to help her stand. Maggie started to slide again when her other shoe found the same slippery substance on the floor.

"Here, sit down," he said, holding on to her as he slid a chair behind her. He used several paper napkins to wipe the cake icing from the soles of her shoes. When he kneeled to slip them back onto her feet, the camera flashed again.

"Well, does the slipper fit?" Kim teased as she joined them.

"Perfectly," Dillon declared with a bow in the direction of the videographer.

"I got it all on tape," the man said happily.

Visions of ending up on a national TV wedding blooper program filled Maggie's head.

"Seriously, are you okay?" Kim asked them both.

"I'm fine. I can't speak for Dillon." Maggie surreptitiously fingered the seams of her gown, hunting for the tear. "Why didn't you just walk over and hand me the bouquet? It would have been much simpler."

Kim grinned. "But not nearly as much fun. That catch will go into the Cornerstone Hall of Fame."

"You mean shame, don't you?" Maggie countered.

"The real shame would have been not having a handsome man around to rescue you."

Maggie's gaze rested on Dillon Rogers. His white teeth flashed, and smile crinkles touched the corners of his eyes as he laughed with Wyatt.

Kim hugged Maggie and said, "We're leaving. Come toss birdseed at us. Just not too hard."

"I'll be right there," she promised. "Let me get the goodie basket the ladies put together for you and Wyatt."

After Kim and Wyatt walked away, Maggie stood. "Dillon." She called his name softly and motioned him over.

"Look at my dress and tell me where it's torn."

She felt more than a little self-conscious as his gaze moved along the lines of the dress. "Pretty color," he commented.

"Same as Mrs. Allene's azaleas," Maggie said.

"I remember," Dillon said. "I look forward to seeing them again next spring."

Did he mean that? Maggie wondered. Spring was seven months away. He'd already stayed for four months when she'd been so sure he would return to his job overseas.

"Ah, here it is," Dillon said. "It's at the top of this slit up the back."

Maggie twisted in an attempt to see the damage.

"It's not noticeable," he assured.

"Thanks. I need to say my good-byes. We still have to put the church back together for services tomorrow."

"Anything I can do to help?"

Maggie paused. "Ask Joe. I'm sure he'd appreciate another strong back."

After waving the bride and groom off in their white limo, Maggie stopped by the bride's dressing room and exchanged her dress for the clothes she'd worn over earlier.

Back in the sanctuary, she collected bows and piled them on the front pew. After completing that task, she found a plastic bag and began picking up the rose petals that littered the aisle.

Dillon found her there when he came back inside.

"Feeling okay?" he asked as he bent to pick up the petals nearest to where he stood and dropped them into the bag.

With renewed humiliation, she said, "I'm fine. Thanks for

trying to help. I hope I didn't hurt you with all that thrashing around."

"No harm done."

❧

Dillon recalled the first time he'd laid eyes on Maggie Gregory. Back in the spring, when he'd come home from Saudi Arabia to care for his ailing mother, he'd been forced to revise his image of Maggie Gregory. He hadn't expected someone closer to his own age, and in all the years his mom had talked about her friend, she'd never thought to share that information with him.

When his mother first mentioned Maggie Gregory, he hadn't recognized the name but figured more than a few things had changed in the more than twenty-five years he'd been away. Then he'd returned home, and when he'd felt those first stirrings of attraction toward his mother's friend, he'd been more than a little uncomfortable. Particularly since he'd had his doubts about the role she played in his mother's life.

"Dillon?" she called, bringing his attention to the bag she held open for the rose petals.

She'd changed into jeans and a T-shirt, her long blond hair still up in the jumble of curls from the wedding. Dillon decided he liked it best flowing about her face and shoulders. She stood nearly as tall as he, making it easy for those bright blue eyes of hers to look deep into his soul.

Why did he become a tongue-tied schoolboy around her? Their stilted conversation was indicative of their relationship. He'd gotten off on the wrong foot with Maggie from day one, and it seemed she didn't plan to let him forget it anytime soon.

"It was a beautiful wedding," Maggie said.

Dillon agreed. It had been interesting seeing yet another of his male friends surrender to marriage. Granted, he'd only known Wyatt for a few months, but Dillon knew Wyatt loved Kim a great deal and felt blessed to have her in his life. Dillon could understand that. Though he'd come to consider himself a committed bachelor over the years, there were times when he wished for someone to love.

Maggie disappeared and returned with the vacuum. "I'll finish up here if you'll find the remembrance table."

As he walked into the fellowship hall, Dillon allowed himself to consider what it would be like to have a wife. Unless he married a much younger woman or one with a ready-made family, there would be no children, but he could see himself happily married at this stage of his life.

"Hey, Dillon, you're a million miles away," Noah said as he and Joe walked past carrying a folded table.

"Maggie needs the remembrance table."

"It's in the hallway outside the office," Joe supplied. "The trays and Bible are on my desk."

"Thanks. Looks like you could use a hand with those."

"Always," Joe Dennis said with a broad grin, adding, "The harvest is truly plenteous, but the laborers are few."

Dillon admired the pastor's ability to quote appropriate scripture for any occasion. "Let me take care of this for her, and I'll be back to help."

Once they had readied the sanctuary for morning services, they moved to the fellowship hall. Maggie went off to help Mari Dennis while Dillon joined the men.

"You can break down tables or fold chairs. Noah and I will haul them to the storage room."

With the help of Kim's dad, they broke down two tables and walked along the hall carrying one on each side.

"Hey, Joe," Noah called to his brother-in-law. "Dillon and Jimmy are carrying twice the workload."

"That means we'll finish in half the time. Then we can get home to eat. You, too, Dillon. You're more than welcome to join us."

"Can I bring anything?"

"No. There's enough food to feed a small army. Though if Mari had her way, we'd probably get chocolate and fruit. She's so disappointed that she missed out on the fountain today," Pastor Joe said. "My idea of comfort food is substantial."

"Yeah, but you have to remember that their comfort with chocolate makes our lives comfortable, too," Noah pointed out. "I buy Julie a box of her favorite chocolates every couple of weeks or so."

The men laughed at his logic as they returned to clearing the room.

ക

"Are you coming back to the house for supper?" Mari asked as they collected the flower arrangements that would be distributed to the elderly congregation members the following morning.

"I'm looking forward to it." Maggie doubted Mari knew how much she appreciated the invitation. She certainly didn't want to go home and sit around by herself tonight.

"Sorry about Luke's commentary at the reception."

"Hey, the kid calls them like he sees them," Maggie said. "I've never been so embarrassed."

"But I saw you laughing."

"I couldn't help myself. During the free-for-all my shoe ended up in some stranger's big purse. You should have seen Dillon's face when he asked for it."

"You two were the highlight of the reception. You've forgiven him?"

Maggie wanted to. She really did. But his accusations had taken her back to a time and place in her life where she didn't want to go. The child who didn't belong anywhere had returned, and she blamed Dillon. Maggie had never imagined that Allene Rogers would leave her anything in her will. She'd tried to make Dillon understand that she had loved his mother a great deal, but he wouldn't listen. His belief that she would take advantage of Mrs. Allene had hurt so much. She had no idea how to explain her feelings to Mari and her other friends. She doubted they would understand any more than she did.

"I'm trying. He's always around," Maggie declared. "He attends my church." She noted Mari's look and said, "Okay, God's church, but he's here. He lives in the house next door. He hangs out with my friends. The only place I don't see Dillon Rogers is at work."

"Let's hope for his sake that's the one place he can avoid."

"Definitely." Maggie wouldn't wish a hospital stay on anyone.

"Joe told me he invited Dillon to supper," Mari said, glancing at her friend as she spoke the words.

A surge of annoyance filled Maggie. Why did the man have to infiltrate her circle of friends? Couldn't he get his own? "That was nice of him."

Mari laughed. "Now that's a diplomatic response if I ever heard one."

Mari carried the box into the kitchen. Maggie followed with the last two vases. "You're pretty accepting of most people's failings. Why not Dillon's?" she asked.

"He sets me on edge. When Mrs. Allene was sick, I only wanted to help her. Then after she died and we learned about the will and house, he treated me like a con artist."

Allene Rogers had been a lifelong member of Cornerstone Community Church. When Maggie came to Myrtle Beach, she moved into Mrs. Allene's rental house. Her new landlord invited her to Cornerstone, and in time, Maggie had become a member. Over the years, the women had grown close. Maggie had cared for Mrs. Allene more as a loving daughter than a neighbor, and the woman had rewarded her by leaving Maggie the rental house in her will.

"He knows you didn't know about the house," Mari said.

After one last look around, they turned out the kitchen lights. They did one last walk-through of the sanctuary and stopped to pick up their dresses. Before plunging the narthex into darkness, Maggie pushed open the front door. The sweltering mid-August heat seemed even hotter after leaving the air-conditioned church.

"I know, but like I said, it's a feeling," Maggie defend...

"Maybe you feel guilty because Mrs. Allene left you the house."

Maybe so, Maggie agreed silently. "He commented on the color of the dresses, and when I said his mom's azaleas were that color, he said he looked forward to seeing them again. You don't think he's planning to stick around that long, do you?"

Mari turned to check the door lock and managed to step on her dress bag.

"Let me carry that before you trip yourself," Maggie offered, taking the long garment bag from her diminutive friend.

"Thanks. Joe said Dillon's enjoying his vacation and considering his plans for the future."

"He hasn't been home since I've known his mother. He flew her and his cousin over there a few times. Mrs. Allene was always so excited because she hadn't seen him in a while," Maggie said. "If my parents were alive, I couldn't imagine not seeing them for weeks, much less years, at a time."

"Men are different than women. A few calls reassure them. Women have to see for themselves."

Maggie shrugged. "But how can his employer afford to give him a year off?"

"I'm sure they have rules in place that address the situation. Will it bother you if he does stay longer?"

"Don't mind me," Maggie said. "I've been out of sorts lately. Let me drop this dress off at the house, and I'll come back to help."

"I'll walk with you," Mari said. Maggie's house was two doors down from the parsonage. "Other than Dillon and the house, what's troubling you?"

"Just having my own little pity party. All my friends have great lives."

"You're still down in the dumps?"

She nodded. Mari had recognized her grief and prayed with Maggie several times since Mrs. Allene's death. "I'm happy for Kim but sad because I know she's going to be busy with her new family."

"Perhaps you need to get out more," Mari suggested. "Find new activities to occupy your time. Joe says the Bible study is popular."

"Maybe I do. Okay, enough of this," Maggie declared. "I'm just feeling sorry for myself. It'll pass."

Mari slipped her arm about Maggie's and said, "Feel free to call when you need to talk. I can't say I remember what being alone is like, but I can listen. And when Kim and Wyatt come home, things will return to normal. You'll see."

Maggie had her doubts. "Thanks for caring, Mari."

"And you don't mind Dillon coming to supper?"

Now why did she have to go and bring that up again? "Why should I mind? It's your house. I don't have to entertain him. We'd better hurry, or there's going to be a house full of guests without a hostess."

Maggie prayed she could work through her discontent. It had been a long time since she'd felt so out of sorts about her life.

two

"It's hot out tonight," Maggie commented, swiping the beads of sweat from her forehead. "I should have worn something cooler than these jeans."

"I hope we don't have a storm later," Mari said. "The twins don't sleep well during thunderstorms."

"That's August for you. Makes me long for fall."

"While the tourists long for endless summers. We took the kids down to the beach earlier in the week. We could hardly find a place to spread out our blanket. Can you believe summer is nearly over?"

"It's flown by. What did you decide about Matt and Mark and school?" Maggie asked. Her friends had been praying over whether they should enroll their two oldest sons in public school or homeschool them. Maggie knew their aunt Julie had offered to pay for a Christian school, but Joe and Mari had refused.

"We're leaning toward homeschooling. It'll be difficult for Matt and Mark to concentrate on their schoolwork with three younger ones running around the house. I'm not sure how we'll get past that."

"It's kindergarten. Give it a try, and if it doesn't work, you can put them in public school next year."

Mari sighed as she opened the screen door leading to her kitchen. "I can't believe how fast they're growing. Seems like yesterday they were keeping me awake half the night."

"Time truly flies," Maggie agreed.

"Any news on the foster parenting application?" Mari asked.

Maggie shook her head. "I don't really expect to hear anything for another month or two."

"Feel free to practice with my kids anytime you feel inclined,"

Mari offered with a laugh. "Then again, that might change your mind about taking on the responsibility."

"I love your kids," Maggie declared as she followed Mari into the house.

"There you are," Julie called as she juggled two large salad bowls. "We were getting ready to send out a search party."

"We took Maggie's things over to her house." Mari reached for her dress, and Maggie draped it over her outstretched arms. "I'll be right back."

"What do you need me to do?" Maggie asked.

"Grab those cups. There's ice in the cooler on the patio. Noah's taking the meat off the grill. There's a slab of ribs for you."

"Oh, I've been craving them forever," she declared. Maggie loved pork ribs. They were messy and not figure friendly, but they were delicious.

A couple of picnic tables covered in festive vinyl cloths sat on the patio area. Mari and Joe had strung fairy lights overhead, and citronella torches flickered about the outer perimeter of the yard, keeping mosquitoes at bay.

Maggie filled cups with ice and poured everyone's beverage of choice. After filling her plate, she opted to sit next to Natalie.

"This seat taken?"

Maggie glanced up to find Dillon standing there. His neatly clipped, mixed gray hair hugged his head, and perfect white teeth flashed as he smiled at them. He had changed into a pair of khaki shorts and a pale blue golf shirt that complemented his tan.

How could he be totally oblivious to her discomfort around him? She'd have thought he would have kept his distance after their earlier escapade. Maggie swallowed quickly and wiped her hands and mouth with her napkin, casting a meaningful glance in Mari's direction before she said, "It's all yours."

He threw one leg over the seat, brushing up against her as

he sat and maneuvered his other leg underneath the table. "Sorry. Never could figure out why the person who invented these things made them so hard to get into."

His comment generated general laughter and agreement around the table.

"I appreciate you inviting me over today," Dillon told Joe. "Nothing better than a meal cooked on the grill."

"I imagine you've had more than your fair share of different foods," Joe said.

"A few. Those look good," Dillon said, eying Maggie's barbecued ribs. He glanced back at the food table. "I didn't see any over there."

Maggie fought the urge to hide her plate. "That's because I'm the only rib fan in the bunch. Noah takes pity on me now and again."

Dillon's gaze drifted toward the plate again. "I haven't had ribs in years."

Since she'd lost her appetite the moment Dillon found his way to her table, Maggie picked up her knife and carved off half of the slab. "Here, take some of these. I can't eat them all."

She didn't add that she generally took home the leftover ribs to enjoy later.

"Don't mind if I do."

He licked his finger and looked at Noah. "You'll have to give me the recipe for this sauce."

"No problem," Noah said with a broad grin. "They sell it in bottles at the grocery store."

Julie punched his arm. "You're supposed to say it's a family secret."

"It is some family's secret," Noah agreed. "Just not mine."

"So what were you talking about before I interrupted?" Dillon asked.

"Mostly we were stuffing our faces," Joe told him.

"I can see why. This food is excellent."

"There's something to be said for big receptions with sit-down dinners," Julie said.

Everyone nodded. Most of them had missed lunch and had only managed small plates of the hors d'oeuvres along with cake and punch.

"Did you hear what Wyatt and Chase gave Kim for a wedding gift?" Julie asked.

Wyatt had redone the kitchen in Kim's condo, and when she agreed to move into his house, he recreated the same kitchen as a wedding gift.

"I'm sure they've heard in some third world countries by now," Noah told his wife. "I thought she was going to have Joe announce it from the pulpit before the wedding."

"Well, I think it's sweet," Julie told him. "That kitchen helped make them a couple."

"But the old rugged cross started it all," Joe said.

Everyone smiled and nodded. Kim had been so thrilled when Cornerstone allowed her to produce the Easter play she'd written. She'd approached Wyatt about building the cross, and they had maneuvered down a long, rocky road that culminated in marriage.

"Wyatt cleans up well," Natalie said.

"I almost didn't recognize him without the work shirts and boots," Maggie admitted.

"Yeah, we all razzed him about that white suit," Noah told the group.

"Isn't it wonderful what men will do for love?" Julie asked, flashing Noah a big smile.

The group chuckled when he leaned to kiss his bride of seven months.

"It was a beautiful wedding," Maggie said, glancing at Natalie. "You outdid yourself with that cake."

Dillon leaned forward and asked, "You made the cake? I thought she'd gotten it from a big city cake designer."

"Thanks," Natalie said. "I lived in New York and worked for one of the best. She taught me a lot, and I taught her a few things in return."

"I can see how," Dillon agreed with a nod. "Hard to

imagine, but it tasted better than it looked. Much better than the groom's cake."

"Don't let Avery hear you say that," Natalie warned.

"Avery?" Dillon asked, looking somewhat puzzled.

"Avery Baker. He made the groom's cake."

"Is he still around?" Dillon asked. "I hung out with his older brother when we were in school. Avery used to drive us crazy following us around and getting us into trouble with his parents."

"Obviously he hasn't changed much," Natalie said in a soft aside to Maggie.

"He owns his parents' bakery now," Mari told Dillon.

"I remember the Bakers. Still, his cake didn't compare to yours."

"Don't tell him that, or you'll elevate my status to arch-enemy number one."

"Over a cake?"

At Dillon's frown, Maggie considered he might have some redeeming qualities after all.

"It's a long story. Suffice it to say that Avery considers me the competition and never lets me forget it."

"You do make an extraordinary cake."

Natalie smiled. "Stop, or you'll make me blush."

He grinned at Natalie, and Maggie felt in the way. Then he winked at Maggie before focusing on his food again. The man used his charm on every woman in sight. She watched as he systematically piled items on his burger and smashed it down before lifting it from the plate. He took a big bite.

"I missed out on the chocolate fountain," Mari said. "I didn't dare risk getting it down the front of my dress."

"Well, break out the bibs," Natalie told her. "I had a cancellation for tomorrow and knew you wouldn't want all that fruit to go to waste."

"Did we tell you we love you?" Maggie asked happily.

"I think you love chocolate more," Natalie teased.

The conversation dropped off as everyone continued to eat.

Maggie ate the wedge of watermelon she'd taken and toyed with the rind. Struck by the silence, she asked, "Where are the kids?"

Mari looked up from her food. "Diana thought taking Chase out would help him not miss Wyatt and Kim as much. She invited Matt, Mark, and Luke along. Robin took the twins over to her house for a while."

"Julie can tell you what a fun experience she's having," Maggie said, winking at her friend.

"I hope Luke doesn't decide to play hide-and-seek," Julie said. "Or sneak Puff along."

Her brother frowned. "No doubt Puff is around somewhere, lying in wait to pounce on some unsuspecting soul."

"Poor Joe," Mari said, rubbing a hand over her husband's shoulders. "He had to climb up and get him out of a tree yesterday. He nearly broke his neck."

"His or the cat's?" Maggie teased, wondering if he'd forgiven his sister for buying the pet without their permission. Mari loved the cat, but Joe often grumbled about the animal's mischievous antics.

Mari grinned at her husband. "His. He said he's calling the fire department next time."

Laughter rippled easily around the table at the thought of their pastor up a tree.

The women followed when Natalie went inside to set up the chocolate fountain. Soon they were stabbing fresh fruit with long skewers and dipping it in the sheets of chocolate that cascaded over the tiered edges of the tower.

The men came inside a few minutes later and laughed at the women as they enthusiastically encouraged each other to try the different items while dodging their efforts to share. They indulged in the cake and chocolate-dipped pretzels Natalie had brought.

Afterward, everyone helped clean up before settling on the patio to sit and talk. The summer evening was abuzz with the concert of frogs and grasshoppers and the scent of honeysuckle in the slight evening breeze.

The Elliotts returned and joined the group. The older boys chased fireflies around the yard, laughing with the abandon of the young. Robin brought the twins home, and they crawled into their parents' laps and fell asleep. All too soon, the wind picked up and the rumble of distant thunder forced them to call it a night.

Natalie stood and announced, "I'm out of here. Thanks for dinner. It was wonderful."

"Me, too," Maggie agreed. "I have to work tomorrow. I'll help with the fountain, Nat."

Dillon stood and said, "Let me help. Thanks for the invite. I'll have to return the favor soon."

After loading the fountain into her car, Natalie drove away and Dillon asked, "Um, Maggie, could I walk you home?"

Surprised by the request, she glanced at him and shrugged. "Sure. Let me get my things."

He followed her back inside and waited while she hugged her friends, said her good nights, and picked up the leftovers she planned to take for lunch the next day.

They walked through the side gate onto the sidewalk running in front of their homes.

"I suppose you're wondering why I asked to walk you home," Dillon said, breaking the noticeable silence.

"What's on your mind?" she asked.

"I think," he said hesitantly then charged forward, "well, don't you think it's time we buried the hatchet and moved onward?"

So long as he didn't want to bury it in her head, Maggie thought wryly.

"It's what Mom would have expected of us. I said things I had no business saying. My mother's property was her business. Not mine."

"I didn't expect it, Dillon."

"I know you didn't. I don't think I ever truly believed any differently. Can we get past this?"

"I'll try if you will."

Even as she spoke the words, Maggie knew she had a ways to go before she could forgive Dillon Rogers. Until she could get past the pain, she didn't know how she could let go of the hurt he'd caused her.

three

On Wednesday morning, Maggie woke early, eager to call Mari and share what had happened the previous day. She fixed breakfast and read the paper while giving her friend time to get the kids settled before making her call.

"I've never been so shocked in my life." Maggie filled her glass from the refrigerator door ice maker and poured freshly made lemonade. She took a long refreshing drink.

"You mean he just walked in and gave you flowers and candy? No, Luke. Let Puff eat. Sorry."

"You sound a bit frazzled," Maggie said.

"They're all in high gear today."

Maggie didn't know how Mari managed with five children under the age of six. "I told him I'd make sure all the nursing staff knew they were from him."

"And that's when he said they were for you?" Mari prompted.

"Exactly," Maggie declared, leaning against the French door and looking into her backyard. The grass needed mowing, and weeds had taken over her flower beds. Maybe this afternoon. Already the heat from the August day radiated against the insulated glass. "You could have knocked me over with a feather."

Mari giggled.

"It's not funny. He said they'd grown very fond of me during his wife's hospitalization."

"They?"

Maggie detected subdued laughter in Mari's tone. "William Smith and his six sons, ages thirteen to eighteen."

"You think he's looking for a working woman to help put them through college?"

Maggie grinned at Mari's comment. "Probably. His wife

23

died two months ago. I refuse to believe he's over her death. I saw the way he took care of her at the hospital. He loved her."

"I'm sure he isn't, but men get on with their lives pretty quickly. Particularly men with six growing boys. So you're truly not interested?"

"He's a nice man but not for me. I thanked him for the flowers and candy, reiterated that I would make sure the entire nursing staff knew they were from him, and said I needed to get back to work."

"How did he take it?"

"He seemed disappointed." Maggie sighed and asked hopefully, "Do you think he got the message?"

"You tell me."

"He'll probably contact me again." William Smith's determined effort to assure she knew the flowers were for her told Maggie he didn't intend to give up easily. "I'm not interested in becoming involved with someone grieving the love of his life. They were married for more than twenty-five years. And I really liked his wife."

"I'm sure it will work out," Mari offered. Maggie could tell she was washing dishes. "You never said why Dillon asked to walk you home the other night."

"Could be he's old-fashioned and didn't want me walking alone at night," Maggie offered evasively.

"Try again."

Maggie sighed and told the truth. "He asked if we could be friends."

Mari burst into laughter. "Oh, this is better than daytime television."

"Hey," Maggie called with mock affront, "this is my life you're laughing at."

"And you don't think it's funny? Just days ago you were down because everyone else had great lives. Now you have two men in pursuit. How do you feel about becoming Dillon's friend?"

"I don't know."

"He's a handsome man. It wouldn't hurt to get to know him better."

"And have my heart broken when he goes back overseas?"

"You said yourself he's not in such a great hurry. Maybe you could change his mind."

"And what if I don't want to change his mind?" Maggie challenged.

"Then you don't. You know we're praying for you to find the right man."

A few months back, their group of friends had agreed to pray for each other to find happiness with the men God intended for them.

"We want you to be happy," Mari said. "The right man will bring you joy you've never known before."

"Pray for Natalie. She's younger and deserves to find her Mr. Right."

"You deserve yours, too."

"You and Julie already meddled once," she reminded.

Maggie hadn't had a clue what Dillon meant when he'd confronted her back in April, saying he'd gotten the message and for her to call off her defenders. She'd been horrified when Mari and Julie admitted they'd talked to Dillon about his behavior.

"We do these things out of love for each other," Mari told her. "What are you doing for lunch? Care to join us for cold ham and potato salad?"

"Sounds. . ." Her words trailed off with the deafening crash. "What on earth?"

"Maggie? What's going on? I hear a horn."

She ran into the living room and paused. Half of the hood of a large old Caddy sat right where her picture window had been. Shattered glass and debris from the front of her house covered the car's hood and littered the floor. Stunned, she noted the car had rammed the sofa where she'd sat reading the paper only minutes before. Where she'd still be if she hadn't gone into the kitchen to call Mari.

The strong odor of gasoline mobilized Maggie into action. She tossed the cordless onto the chair and moved cautiously toward the vehicle. Though she couldn't be sure from the way he was slumped against the steering wheel, Maggie suspected the driver to be Max Carter. She knew him from church.

"Maggie? Where are you?" Dillon Rogers's horrified cry gave her pause. He yelled again, sounding frantic.

She panicked when Dillon began ripping away boards. She had no idea whether the car would continue to move once the barricades were removed.

"Stop!" Maggie screamed.

Doubtful he could hear her over the car's engine and blaring horn, Maggie considered her options.

Praying all the while that the car wouldn't lurch forward and kill her, Maggie grabbed the chenille throw from the recliner. Bits of glass fell to the floor as she gave it a quick shake then used it to brush the remaining glass from the car hood. She barely felt the warm metal as she crawled through the opening to reach the passenger side door. Tears of joy sprang to her eyes when it opened easily. She entered the vehicle, turned the key, and sighed in relief when the revving engine sputtered once, then twice, and died.

Maggie turned her attention to Max, checking his vitals and determining he was no longer with them. Tears trailed down her cheeks as she sent up a prayer for his family.

"Are you trying to get yourself killed?"

Taking Dillon's anguished question in stride, she gently shifted Max's body to lean his head back against the seat. The horn ceased blaring. She closed his eyes before backing out the passenger door. "I had to do something before you ripped those boards away."

Dillon pulled her into his arms. "You took ten years off my life."

"Couldn't you hear the engine?" she asked, not minding that he held her.

"I thought he'd hit you. I saw you sitting on the sofa when

I went out to the mailbox earlier."

"I was in the kitchen."

"Thank God." His heartfelt declaration shook her to the bottoms of her feet.

Despite the August heat, Maggie trembled from shock.

"It's okay," he comforted, hugging her again.

She remained within the confines of his arms until Mari's and Joe's cries reached her ears.

"Over here," Dillon called.

"I need to call an ambulance."

"What happened?" Mari called.

"Max drove into the house. He's dead."

Mari gasped.

"He just left the church," Joe said. "He wasn't feeling well."

"They're sending an officer and an ambulance," Dillon said after he used his cell phone to speak with the 911 dispatcher. Dillon wrapped his arm about Maggie's waist and guided her around the vehicle and out into the yard, relinquishing his hold to Mari. "She's in shock," he said softly before walking over to talk with Joe.

"Oh, Mari, Max is dead," she said and burst into tears.

"Shh, it's okay," her friend comforted. "Thank God you're safe."

Maggie swiped her eyes and said, "What's wrong with me? I never cry."

"I think having a car driven into your house is reason enough. Thank God you were in the kitchen."

"Linda will be devastated," Maggie declared sadly. She knew Max's wife from the church nursery, and they had talked many times about her husband's refusal to see a doctor.

"When I came into the living room, the car hood was half in the house with the engine running and the horn blaring. Dillon was yelling my name." Maggie's voice broke as she gulped in a deep breath and shook harder at the memory. "I suppose he's thinking it serves me right," she murmured, feeling guilty the moment the words passed her lips. He'd obviously been very concerned when he came to her rescue. "I'm sorry. He doesn't deserve that."

"No, he doesn't," Mari admonished. "Why would you even think that? This unforgiving woman isn't the Maggie I know."

Her comments hit Maggie like a dousing of ice water on a hot summer day. It had never been her intention to behave so poorly toward another of God's children.

Joe and Dillon walked up, and Dillon said, "Why don't you come over to the house and sit on the porch?"

"I need to stay here."

"It was the most awful noise," Mari told them, describing what she'd heard over the phone.

Their gazes turned to the police car as it pulled into the driveway, siren blaring and blue lights flashing. A fire truck followed.

Mari greeted the officer, another member of Cornerstone.

"Mrs. Dennis. Pastor Dennis. What happened, Miss Gregory?"

Before Maggie could tell him, the ambulance arrived. She turned away when the attendants removed Max's body from the car and took him away to be officially pronounced. As a nurse, she'd witnessed death before. Maggie had no idea why it bothered her so much this time. Burt pulled out his notepad and began asking questions.

Minutes later, a wrecker arrived and slowly pulled the car from the home. The large car cleared the house, taking out one of the porch supports, and the A-frame of the roof slapped against the front with a thud.

"We should have shored up the roof," Dillon told Joe.

The car retreated across what had once been a well-landscaped lawn, leaving the fountain and statuary in shambles. Maggie considered how long she'd searched for those pieces and how thrilled she'd been when Kimberly called to say she'd found exactly what Maggie wanted.

Now their loss was nothing compared to the tragic loss of Max's life. Fresh tears welled in Maggie's eyes, and Mari wrapped her arms about her friend. Maggie groaned when the television van pulled up behind the officer's car just as the fire truck and ambulance pulled away.

"I'll handle this, Miss Gregory," Burt said, walking over to greet the reporter. They shot footage and then left the scene after getting a statement from the officer.

"Max's fifteen minutes of fame," Maggie whispered.

"It is more than we're used to on Maple Street," Joe said.

The officer returned. "Sorry about that. They heard it on the scanner."

"Thanks for keeping me off camera," Maggie told him.

"I didn't want them releasing anything until we notify Max's wife."

"Can I come along when you do that?" Joe asked.

"I'd appreciate it, Pastor Joe. That's one of my least favorite job tasks."

"Mine, too."

"I think that does it, Miss Gregory." He ripped off a piece of the form and handed it to her. "You'll need this for your insurance. Have a nice day," he said, tipping his head politely before he walked over to the cruiser.

Just how does he suppose I do that? Maggie wondered. Struggling to regain her composure, she asked, "Where are the kids?"

"With Noah."

Joe came over and said, "I'm going with Burt to notify Linda Carter. Maggie, I'll come back later to help secure your house."

"I'd better get back to the kids. Will you be okay?" Mari asked Maggie.

"I'm fine."

Dillon stepped up beside her. "I'll stay."

Mari nodded and asked Maggie, "Will you come to the house for lunch?"

"I have to secure everything first."

"We'll take care of it for you," Dillon promised with a caring smile.

Maggie's heart thumped.

Mari moved to the sidewalk and looked back once more, waving good-bye. Maggie waved listlessly in return.

"Why don't you go with her and call your insurance agent?" Dillon suggested.

"I need to take care of my home."

"You need to know what your agent wants you to do," Dillon said. "I'll stay here and keep watch. Do you have any tarps? We need them for the roof."

Maggie shook her head.

"We'll find some. I have plywood. And we need to make sure the house is safe to enter."

"Thanks, Dillon." The adrenaline that had pumped through her minutes earlier had evaporated, leaving nothing but feelings of sadness behind.

He looked at her for what seemed a long time. "It'll be okay, Maggie. We'll have it sorted out in no time. A couple of boards over the opening and you'll be safe and secure."

Maggie didn't know how secure she'd feel with a bit of lumber keeping intruders at bay. She rubbed her hands over her face, images of Max Carter and the car coming clearly to mind.

"Once the insurance adjustor gets the claim processed, we can get contractors in and have the place looking better than ever," Dillon continued.

It would be so nice to drop all this on him, but Maggie didn't feel that was fair. "You're busy with your place."

He'd spent the last couple of months updating the house that had been around since the thirties.

"It will be okay, Maggie. I promise."

She smiled at him. "I'm sorry, Dillon. Truly I am."

"For what?"

"The way I've treated you. You don't deserve my anger. You had every right to feel I'd stolen your inheritance."

Dillon looked shocked. "Don't say that. This house belonged to my grandparents. They gave Mom and Dad the house next door when they married, so it's not as if they worked themselves to death for their land. And I don't think I did anything to deserve my inheritance, either. Nothing beyond having the good fortune to be my parents' son."

A pained look spread across her face.

"What is it, Maggie? What did I say?"

"I was my parents' daughter. And then they were gone, and I was nobody's child. I lived in foster homes from the time I was eleven years old. The Floyds and your mom were the only adults besides my parents who ever made me feel truly at home. I didn't help Mrs. Allene because I wanted something from her. I loved her."

Dillon enveloped her in his arms and whispered, "Shh. I know. I'm sorry, too, Maggie. I hurt you with my accusations. I know you loved Mom. The house doesn't matter to me. It was fear that I'd allowed someone to take advantage of my elderly parent. Guilt because I hadn't been bothered to care for her myself."

"Why didn't you come home earlier?"

"I wish I had."

Maggie wished he had, too. She regretted that he'd missed his mother's last years. "I'll never be too busy to help you, Maggie. Go make your call," he said when she looked at the house again.

Dillon settled into the swing hanging beneath the shade of the old gnarled tree. If only the car had veered a couple of feet to the left, it would have struck the tree rather than the house. "I'll wait here."

"I'll be right back."

"Take a few minutes," he advised gently. "You're still in shock."

Maggie supposed she was. She trembled and felt chilled despite the sun. "I don't want to impose."

"It's not imposing. It's called being neighborly."

"Can I at least offer you a glass of lemonade?" He raised his brows as if asking how she planned to accomplish that.

"The back door is unlocked. I can go around the house."

"I'm fine. Go make your call so we'll know how to proceed."

She took a couple of steps and then turned back, dropping onto the seat beside him. "It just occurred to me that I don't have insurance on the house. The estate isn't settled. I have content insurance."

Dillon thought for a minute or two. "Home owners probably won't cover it anyway. Max Carter's vehicle insurance should."

"Then I should call his company?" Maggie fished the insurance information Burt had given her from her pocket and named the national company listed there.

"Let's call Mom's agent and have him advise us."

"I have the same agent," Maggie volunteered. "Mrs. Allene told me about him when I rented the house."

"Do you have the number?"

"In my purse. Inside the house."

"Tell you what," Dillon said. "You stay here and take it easy. I'll grab the phone book."

❧

As Dillon ran across to his house, he understood Maggie's confusion more and more. Seeing that old Caddy in her house had been the ultimate shock for him.

He forced himself to breathe more slowly when fear swamped him again. She could have been killed. And he would have cared.

Dillon admitted the truth to himself. He'd grown fond of Maggie Gregory. She might be as prickly as a cactus, but she had a good heart. He knew he had to help her get past the hurt he'd caused. He'd do it, too. No doubt, she'd give him fits, but he knew the end result would make it worthwhile.

❧

After Dillon disappeared inside his house, Maggie dropped a foot to the ground and gave the swing a push. So many things filled her head—Max's death, Mari's words of admonishment, Dillon's caring. Why did she doubt his intentions? He'd done nothing to make her believe he wanted anything more than to help her through a trying situation.

"Maggie."

She smiled at Julie and Noah Loughlin. Julie hugged her. "Are you okay? I know I'd be freaked out if a car drove into the front of our place."

The idea made Maggie giggle. They lived in a second floor beach condominium. "Let's hope no car ever gets that high."

Julie and Noah smiled.

"What will you do?" Noah asked.

"Dillon's getting the phone. It's such a mess. The house is tied up with the estate, and we don't know whether to call the home owner or vehicle agent."

"I'd say the vehicle," Julie volunteered.

Noah nodded agreement. "You may have to get the home-owner's agent involved before it's over, but Max's insurance is definitely liable."

"How's Linda?" Maggie asked.

"Joe's with her now."

"I feel so bad for her," Maggie said in an almost whisper. "She wanted him to see a doctor, but he refused. Said it was indigestion."

"Men can be so stubborn," Julie agreed, glancing at her husband.

"Hey, we don't have a monopoly on stubborn. You're pretty stubborn, too, Mrs. Loughlin."

Julie grimaced at him, and Maggie watched the couple's loving playfulness and wondered what life would be like with someone who loved her that much.

"Noah's going to come over later and help board up the house. Are you sure it's safe to be inside?"

"I don't know," Maggie said.

"Dillon, hi," Julie called when she saw him walking toward them. "A bit too much excitement in the neighborhood, I hear."

"You're not kidding." He passed Maggie the phone book. "Give me the agent's name, and I'll call him for you."

"I can talk to him."

"Like you said, the estate isn't settled, so he'll probably have to talk to me anyway."

Maggie didn't feel like arguing, so she flipped to the yellow pages and calmly recited the agent's office number.

Dillon dialed and a few minutes later told her they could do what they needed to secure the house until the adjustor could get there. "He said he'd be over shortly to take pictures. Turns out he has Max Carter's car insurance, too."

He glanced at Noah and said, "We need tarps to cover the roof. If we pile the worst of the debris out of the way, we should be able to secure the front with plywood."

"That doesn't sound very safe," Julie offered.

"Mom always said locks only keep honest people out," Noah pointed out.

"But still. . . ," Julie began, cutting off at her husband's warning look. "You can stay with us."

"Thanks, but I'd just as soon stay here," Maggie said. "Perhaps thieves will be less inclined to break in if I'm here. I can take some personal days."

"Noah and I will help in every way possible," Julie said.

"Me, too," Dillon promised.

As she sat and studied the devastation to her home, her thoughts centered even more on the Carter family. Her loss seemed minute compared to theirs. They'd lost their beloved husband and father.

"Dear Lord," she whispered, "please be with Linda and her family as they deal with the loss of their loved one. Help them to find great joy in knowing Max was Your child and has gone home to be with You.

"And please help me let go of the pain and anger that keep me from being the witness You would have me be. Amen."

four

The insurance adjustor finally showed up on Friday and determined the majority of the damage was limited to the house front. Dillon's structural engineer friend had basically said the same thing on Thursday.

Dillon made a long list of things for her to ask but came over when the man arrived and recounted every item. If the adjustor found Dillon's actions puzzling, he didn't say anything. He just jotted on his forms and did the math. When the totals were completed, Maggie was shocked to learn there was more than twenty thousand dollars' damage to her house and gardens.

Everything added up—the structure, furniture replacement, landscaping, and labor. The list seemed endless. Maggie's head was spinning by the time the adjustor told her he'd get a check in the mail.

"What about damage that might not be found until the work gets under way?" Dillon asked.

"Here's my card," the man said, handing it to Maggie. "Give me a call if anything comes up."

"Unbelievable," Maggie said after he'd driven off. "For a few minutes there, I thought he was going to declare the place totaled."

Dillon smiled. "I'm sure he deals with far more vehicle collisions than house and car. So where do you want to start?"

"I don't know."

"We need a contractor. Anyone from church you do business with?"

Maggie shook her head. "I'll ask around and see if I can get a recommendation."

"Want me to handle this for you? I can call the contractors.

See what they say."

"You don't have time."

"Sure I do. Now that we know the place isn't going to fall down on your head, we can take our time and do it right."

"Not too long, I hope," Maggie offered quickly. Somehow the very thought of repairing the house front as quickly as possible made her hope she could forget the incident that plagued her still.

The living room might be usable, but she found the darkness depressing. Plywood obstructed sunlight that had flooded the room. She couldn't even welcome visitors at her front door. They had to come around the house and enter through the back.

She'd spent Wednesday night on the sofa in Mari and Pastor Joe's study. Despite Julie's invitation, she hadn't felt right about intruding on the newlyweds. Thursday night, she'd spent a restless, nightmare-filled night in her own bed. She prayed her anxiety would stop soon.

"Depends on how busy they are," Dillon said. "We want recommendations from past jobs. I think we can get the work under way soon enough. That is, if you'll trust me to do this for you."

She looked at him, seeing the question in his expression. "I do trust you, Dillon, and I appreciate everything you've done for me. But I don't feel right about dumping my responsibility on your shoulders."

"When do you work again?"

"Tomorrow. I'm on the night shift this week."

"Why don't I make a couple of calls and see if we can get someone out today? I doubt anyone's available, but it can't hurt to try."

After Dillon left, Maggie went inside and sorted laundry. He returned just as she was taking her uniforms from the washer. "What did you find out?"

"Pretty much what we thought. One guy can come by tomorrow."

Maggie sighed and reminded, "Max's funeral is in the morning."

"Let me help," Dillon requested again. "Give me a key. We'll look at the house and lock up after we finish."

"It's too much to ask," Maggie declared with a shake of her head. "You can't finish your place if you're working on mine."

"My house is at a stopping point. And I won't be doing the work myself," he insisted. "Just supervising. Carrying out your decisions."

Maggie didn't understand why Dillon made it sound almost critical that he do this. "But you're on vacation. You don't want to spend your time off working. What about your job?" she asked. "If you get called back before the house is finished, I won't have a clue what to do."

"I'll keep you informed every step of the way," Dillon said. "And I won't be called back."

"You've been here for months, Dillon. Surely your employer doesn't plan for you to remain on leave indefinitely."

"Actually, I retired. I notified them a couple of months after I came home."

Surprise filled her. "I thought you liked your work."

"I did, but I don't want to go back. I don't have to work."

"Then you're a very fortunate man." Early retirement wasn't in her future. She hoped to increase her retirement plan contributions now that she didn't have to pay rent, but that had to wait until after she'd sorted out tax and insurance costs. "I'm sure you worked hard to get to that point," she added.

"So you'll let me help?"

She shook out another uniform top, slipped it on a hanger, and hung it on the rod over the utility sink. "You'll let me know if it gets to be too much?" she questioned.

"We'll get everything knocked out in a week or two, and you'll be back to normal before you know what happened."

"I'll be in your debt."

"No charge," he said softly.

She looked up, and their gazes caught and held. The idea

that something of great import had just happened grabbed hold and refused to let go. He smiled and she smiled back.

"Now, how about we go out to lunch. I have a taste for seafood."

She glanced at the washer. "I need to do a couple more loads."

"It's just lunch," he offered. "Unless you want to run by the hardware store and look at windows and doors."

She was hungry. And she could do laundry this afternoon as easily as now. "Give me time to brush my hair."

He glanced at his watch. "I'll meet you out front in fifteen minutes."

"Better give me thirty. I have to finish here."

"Go comb your hair," he said, reaching for a wet shirt. "I'll do this."

"No!" Maggie cried, horrified by the idea of leaving Dillon to handle her laundry.

"Okay," he declared, stepping away. "Thirty minutes."

He must think I'm crazy, Maggie thought as she pinned pants onto a hanger. But there was something too personal about allowing the man to handle her garments.

Dillon was getting very personal. Maggie considered the way he'd pursued helping her with the house. And now offering to hang up her laundry. . . She definitely felt confused by his behavior.

In her bedroom, she glanced down at the clothes she wore and decided to change. She didn't know where he planned to lunch but decided a pair of capri pants and sleeveless top in a rose color would probably be fine.

After changing, she brushed her hair and slid on a pair of sandals, all the while keeping an eye on the clock. Ready with a couple of minutes to spare, she secured the back door and walked over to where Dillon waited by his mother's car.

"You look nice," he said, holding the car door open for her.

"Thank you," she returned, both for the compliment and gentlemanly gesture.

He walked around and slid behind the wheel. Mrs. Allene's car was a fully loaded, newer model, far more advanced than Maggie's economy car. She'd always found it very comfortable. Dillon had cooled the interior while waiting for her.

Thinking he'd name one of a multitude of local restaurants, Maggie asked, "So where did you have in mind for lunch?"

"I'm thinking Calabash. That okay with you?"

She knew the little town just off the North Carolina border well. They had a reputation for being crazy about seafood, and Maggie had eaten more than her share of "Calabash-style" seafood.

So much for an hour for lunch. The drive there would take almost that long. "Sure," Maggie agreed. "I just need to get back in time for Max's visitation tonight."

At least she had clothes to wear tomorrow. She'd planned to grocery shop, but she could pick up something from the cafeteria.

"Mom loved Calabash."

"Yes, she did. How does it feel to be eating American again?"

"My waist is bearing the brunt of it," he said with a laugh. "If I keep eating like this, I'll have to buy new clothes."

Maggie considered his trim appearance. She felt certain he was one of those people who could eat anything and never gain weight. She should be so fortunate. "What was the food like there?"

"Different but good. Lamb and grilled chicken were staples. I'll have to prepare some of my favorites and let you be the judge."

"Sounds like fun," Maggie agreed. "Where did you live?"

"In Riyadh, the capital. The company has a private compound with a pool, small store, book and video libraries, even a barbershop."

Maggie found Dillon to be quite an accomplished storyteller as he spoke of his years in Saudi Arabia.

Upon their arrival, he parked and then escorted her inside

the restaurant. After they were seated, Maggie picked up their conversation where it had left off. "What made you choose to live there?"

He paused for a moment then said, "A woman."

Her head went crazy with thoughts of unrequited love that might have driven a man like Dillon Rogers to such a place to overcome his pain.

"We met in our third year at NC State and dated for years. I thought one day we'd marry and come back to live next door to my parents.

"Needless to say, she didn't feel the same way. When she accused me of not having an adventurous bone in my body, I took the job in Saudi to prove her wrong. I fell out of love with her and in love with the challenges of my new life and didn't look back. Last I heard, she's living in some little one-horse town with her third or fourth husband."

"Did she ever contact you again?"

"I think Mom forwarded a letter sometime between husbands two and three."

"Is she the reason you never married?"

Dillon rested his arm over the back of the chair next to him. "I don't think so. Every now and again, the idea of a wife and family appealed, but I didn't want to give up my job and move back to the States."

"Weren't there families over there?"

"Yeah," he said with a nod. "Some of the guys were married. Even had children. I didn't want that life for my family."

"Do you have regrets?"

He shrugged. "A few. Mostly when I hear people talking about their kids and grandkids. I know it probably disappointed my parents that I didn't produce an heir to carry on the Rogers family name. But there are male cousins with boys, so the name continues."

No doubt, Mrs. Allene would have adored a couple of grandchildren for reasons other than preserving the family name. She'd loved kids, particularly Pastor Joe and Mari's bunch.

"What about you? You never married, either. Why?"

Turnabout was fair play. He'd answered her question and now awaited her answer. Did she really want to tell him fear had kept her from falling in love?

"My mom died when I was very young, and then my dad died when I was eleven. There was no family left, so I ended up in the foster care system. I lived in a few homes, but when I turned fourteen, they placed me with the Floyds. They were a loving couple, and I was the only foster child they ever had."

"They never adopted you?"

"No, but I'm thankful for all they did for me. The money from the state stopped when I turned eighteen. They had no obligation, but they wanted me to get my education. I chose to become a registered nurse because of my foster mother."

"Do you stay in touch with them?"

"We talk on the phone. They live in a retirement village just outside DC."

"So why didn't you marry?" he asked again.

"I wanted a family, to be loved, but I was too afraid to make it happen."

"What made you afraid?" Dillon asked.

"I could never get it just right." Maggie could tell her comment baffled him. "Like the three bears, I was either too this or too that in every relationship."

"So the men moved on?"

Maggie nodded. "To women who were less complicated. Then I moved here, and your mom invited me to Cornerstone. I found contentment in my Lord and Savior that I'd never known before. I didn't feel as alone anymore. I had my new family at Cornerstone, and everything was wonderful."

"Until I showed up?"

"Everything fell apart when Mrs. Allene got sick," Maggie admitted. "Like God and Cornerstone, your mother had become a stabilizing influence in my life. When I felt depressed, Mrs. Allene prayed for me and helped me accept that things wouldn't always be so bad. When I needed to talk, she listened. And when I needed good advice, she gave it."

Dillon nodded slowly. "Sounds like Mom. She refused to allow me to feel sorry for myself. I remember the times she told me to get a backbone."

"Ouch."

He grinned. "She could be tough when she needed to be. And I suspect having me as a son made that need surface rather often. She never sent me to talk to Dad. She had her own discussions, making what she would and would not tolerate very clear.

"We butted heads on lots of issues, but I knew she loved me. I never realized how much until I took the Saudi job and she didn't try to change my mind. Told me I needed to finish growing up." A poignant smile touched his face. "It's tough when you're nearly thirty years old and your mom says you need to grow up. But I knew she was right."

"Did you feel abandoned?"

"No. Mom sent care packages, and we talked regularly. She helped direct my path, just as she'd always done, except she did it from thousands of miles away.

"When Dad died and I came home for the funeral, I considered coming back for good, but she told me not to do it for her. Said she didn't need me giving up the life I loved to come home and make us both miserable," Dillon said with a distant smile.

"That explains her resistance to calling you when she got sick."

He looked surprised. "She didn't want to call?"

Maggie shook her head slowly. "Told me to mind my own business when I said it wasn't fair to you."

"She'd do that," he agreed, sadness touching his expression. "I wish she'd told me sooner."

"I should have known things weren't right with her," Maggie said. "Should have seen how sick she was. Maybe she'd still be alive if I had."

"Sounds like she protected you, too."

The waitress arrived with platters of hot seafood, French fries, coleslaw, and hush puppies. Dillon said grace and they started to eat.

Maggie considered what he'd said. How long had Mrs. Allene known she had a terminal illness? "Kim's mom said Mrs. Allene needed time to strengthen herself."

"Maybe it's a mom thing," Dillon said. "She didn't want me to grieve her loss before I had to."

"We're all creatures of habit. We hide our emotions behind brick walls and don't let our loved ones see how much we're hurting when life could be so much easier if we shared the load."

"Do you think mankind will ever catch on?"

Maggie shook her head. "No. We'll keep on bumbling our way through. That's human nature. I'm sorry I didn't call earlier."

Dillon laid his fork on the plate and wiped his mouth. "I need to admit something. After you called, I had problems believing things were as bad as you indicated. I felt Mom would have told me if that were the case. Still I couldn't get what you said off my mind and called my cousin Leslie. Once she told me how sick Mom was, I caught the next plane home.

"I'm sorry, Maggie. I suppose I should have kept that to myself, but since the subject of communication came up, I think it's important that you know. I don't want to risk it coming up later and hurting even more."

"I don't blame you," she said, her voice raspy with emotion. "I was a stranger."

Dillon covered her hand with his and squeezed. "You were Mom's friend. You were there. I should have listened."

"I wondered why you were being so bullheaded," Maggie told him. "I was positive you'd realize your mother was trying to protect you."

He shook his head. "When Mom said she was okay, I believed her."

Maggie understood his distress. She'd felt the exact same way when Mrs. Allene told them to stay out of her business. "Don't beat yourself up, Dillon. You were there in time. That's all that matters."

"I could have been a better son."

"You can't change the past. Mrs. Allene got what she wanted. You didn't sit around watching her die. She couldn't bear the thought of that."

"But she allowed you to be there," he pointed out.

"I didn't ask permission," Maggie told him. "I kept showing up, and she was too weak to throw me out."

"Thanks, Maggie. For everything."

She nodded and watched Dillon for a few moments as he returned to his meal. Dillon Rogers had grown into a fine man. Mrs. Allene would be proud of her son.

five

Maggie had many things on her mind when she returned to work the following day—the Carter family's grief, Dillon's lunch revelations, and her home repairs. Finding yet another flower arrangement from her admirer only added to the mix. "When did they arrive?"

"Around lunchtime. Who sent them?" her coworker asked.

Praying she was wrong, Maggie reached for the card. Just as she'd suspected. "Would you believe William Smith?"

"You mean the man who lost his wife a couple of months ago? Are you dating?"

"No," Maggie denied hotly. "I don't date." Although yesterday with Dillon had been like a date. The first one she'd been on in years. "Mr. Smith sent flowers and candy last week. I left them for the staff."

"So he's interested in you?"

"How can he be interested in anyone? You saw how much he loved his wife."

"Maybe he doesn't like being alone," Belinda said with a shrug. "He wouldn't be the first."

"I'm not interested. I tried to tell him, but I don't think he got the message."

"He has nice taste in flowers."

Belinda fingered the large sunflowers in the massive arrangement that held so many colorful summer flowers.

"Take them home with you," Maggie offered.

Belinda asked, "You sure?" At Maggie's nod, she said, "Okay, I will. How were your days off?"

"You wouldn't believe me if I told you," Maggie said with a grim smile.

"What happened?"

45

"A car drove into my house. Right into my living room."

"That was you? I saw it on the news. Poor Maggie. You're blessed that you weren't killed."

She shuddered. "When I consider I was sitting on the sofa not fifteen minutes before. . . If I hadn't gone into the kitchen to make a call. . ."

Maggie drew a deep breath. "I feel so bad for the man's family. His wife works in the church nursery with me occasionally. The funeral was today."

"That's right. The driver died."

Maggie nodded. "He had a heart attack."

Belinda shook her head in disbelief. "What are you doing about the repairs to your house?"

"My neighbor is handling things."

"The one whose mother owned the place?"

Maggie nodded. "He's agreed to help me find a contractor and get things straightened out."

"That's nice of him."

Very, Maggie agreed silently. She just wished she didn't feel so suspicious of Dillon's motives.

"I know that's a gigantic weight off your shoulders." Belinda yawned. "We'd better get through this before I fall asleep. Madison has been feverish and cranky for a couple of days now."

"Did it occur to you to call in sick?"

"Bobby took care of her last night and said she's better today. Hopefully we'll have her back in day care on Monday."

Belinda launched into a summary of the day's activities. After she left, Maggie reviewed charts and started her routine of checking in with the patients and carrying out the doctors' orders. One patient went off for a test, three more were admitted, and before she realized it, suppertime had arrived.

As she ate her sandwich, Maggie wondered about the outcome of the contractor's visit but restrained herself from calling Dillon. She'd promised to trust him and felt certain he'd let her know.

By morning, she was glad to see her replacement arrive. Just as she was finishing for the day, a nurse from emergency called up to say a woman was asking for her.

Wondering who it could be, Maggie grabbed her purse, called good-bye, and headed for the elevator. In the ER, she stopped by the desk, and the attendant pointed to the seats along the side of the room. She recognized Mrs. Pearson and a screaming Chloe Turner from church. She hurried over to where they sat.

"Maggie, thank God you're here!" the woman cried.

Chloe's wails had everyone in the waiting area looking at them with raised brows. She lifted the little girl from Mrs. Pearson's arms and whispered a few soothing words as she patted the baby's back. Soon Chloe's sobs became hiccups. "What's going on? Why are you here with Chloe? Where's Peg?"

Maggie knew Peg Turner rented Mrs. Pearson's garage apartment. Peg's husband had left her for another woman a few months before.

"I hadn't seen her in a couple of days, and I thought I'd better check on them," Mrs. Pearson explained as she patted the child's shoulder. "Peg was so sick. I called an ambulance. Chloe and I followed in my car."

Maggie rocked gently, soothing the little girl. "Did you bring her bottle or a diaper bag?"

"I didn't think about that. Everything happened so fast."

Maggie glanced down, relieved to find the little girl had drifted off to sleep. "Take her and let me check on Peg. I'll be right back."

Peg was indeed very sick. She had a ruptured appendix and would be staying in the hospital for a few days.

"Maggie, where's Chloe? Why is she crying?"

"Mrs. Pearson has her in the lobby. She's fine. Don't worry. We'll take care of her during your hospital stay."

"I can't stay," Peg protested weakly, trying to rise from the bed. "I have to take care of Chloe."

Maggie rested a hand against her shoulder, holding her

still. "Peg, you have to get better to do that. I'll be happy to take Chloe home with me if that's okay with you. She knows me from the church nursery. And I'll let Pastor Dennis know what's going on with you. I'm sure he'll stop by."

"You won't let them take her away?"

The fear in Peg's softly spoken question tugged at Maggie's heart. She had no doubt the single mother worried about what would happen to her child if she weren't around to care for her.

"Your church family will take good care of Chloe," Maggie promised. "You'll be back at home with her before you know it."

The woman sagged weakly against the bed. "Thanks, Maggie. I was so afraid. Mrs. Pearson has a key to the apartment. She can let you in to get what you need for Chloe. She's a good baby."

Maggie listened as Peg weakly outlined a few basics for caring for her child before insisting, "You rest now. I'll check on you tonight."

Sometime later, Maggie carried the baby into her house. She had scarcely gotten inside when Dillon knocked on the door.

"Where have you been? I thought you'd be home. . ." His voice trailed off as his gaze rested on the sleeping baby in her arms.

"Something came up," Maggie told him. "Here, hold her while I get some bedding."

"Uh, Maggie," Dillon muttered uncomfortably when she placed the child in his stiff arms and adjusted them into a cradle.

"Oh come on, Dillon. She's asleep. Just hold on to her. Here, sit down. You'll feel more comfortable."

"Whose baby is this?" he asked when she started to walk away.

"I'll fill you in once I get her settled."

"Maggie!" Dillon called in alarm when she started to leave the room.

"Shush," Maggie warned. "You'll wake her."

Dillon glanced down and back at Maggie with total uncertainty in his expression.

"You're doing fine," she said. "I'll be right back."

Maggie folded and tucked bedding until she'd made a small pallet on the floor. She lifted the child from Dillon's hold, shushing Chloe when she woke briefly.

"Whew." She blew out a deep breath and dropped back on the chair arm. She noted Dillon watching her, allowing his gaze to drop to the sleeping baby before coming back to her.

Weary, she rubbed her face and explained how she'd been called to the ER after work to find Chloe crying so loud she had everyone in the waiting room cringing. "She stopped when I took her."

"So where's her mom?"

"In the hospital. Peg's very sick. I promised to take care of Chloe until she's released."

"How can you do that and work, too?" Dillon asked.

"I have a plan. Don't look at me like that," she said defensively. "It was the right thing to do."

"And you need one more thing to take up your time, I suppose?" Dillon asked.

"She's not a thing. She's a baby."

"I know, but with your job and now the house situation, wouldn't it be better if someone else cared for her? Maybe Mari Dennis."

"Mari doesn't need another child, Dillon. She has five of her own. Chloe is comfortable with me, and I promised Peg."

"She'll probably keep you awake all day."

"It wouldn't be the first time I've lost a bit of sleep," Maggie assured.

"Where's her father?"

"Peg said he spends his time barhopping and getting himself into trouble. He doesn't even pay child support. You think I should entrust Chloe to him?"

"He's her father. Maybe taking responsibility for his child

would force him to rethink his life."

Maggie refused to consider contacting the man. "Peg's already lost her husband and her home. I won't let anything happen to Chloe. She stays right here with me until her mother can take over."

He looked thoroughly chastised. "Okay, I'm sorry. You're right. I just thought maybe we could go to dinner later and talk about the contractor."

"Losing your mom is a big deal when you're grown, but you'll have to admit it's even bigger when you're Chloe's age," Maggie said. "If you really want to go out, I can handle a baby at a restaurant. But you're welcome to eat with us. I have spaghetti sauce defrosting in the fridge and thought I'd make garlic bread."

"She won't be a happy camper when she wakes up and finds her mom missing."

Maggie found it interesting that Dillon had already determined what Chloe would be like when she woke. "She'll be fine. Did the contractor show up yesterday?"

He looked disgusted. "Yeah, he came. Two hours after he said he'd be here. Didn't offer any explanation for being late. No apology. Poked around for another hour and said he can't start work until late September."

Maggie's brows lifted at that. "Why so long? I'd hoped that with his quick response, he'd be available right away."

"After talking to him, I don't think he could handle the job anyway."

"Really? Why?"

"He couldn't give me references, and there was something about his attitude. He got too excited when I mentioned you wanted the job completed as quickly as possible.

"I think he's saying late September so we'd feel we should pay him more when he moves you up on the schedule. He kept asking about overtime. And his quote was on the high side. I went over to see Wyatt."

"Was Kim there?"

"At the store. Chase was hanging out at the shop with his dad. All he could talk about was Florida."

Maggie laughed. "He's excited about the trip."

"Wyatt's going to give me the name of a couple of contractors he knows. And he'll do what he can to help get things sorted out when he gets back."

"That's sweet of him."

Dillon studied her for a moment. "You didn't say it was sweet of me."

Maggie smiled. "How do you know? Maybe I've told everyone that you're wonderful for doing this."

He shrugged. "Maybe you have. You should get some rest. What can I do to help?"

"Could you pick up the playpen from Mari's after church? She said Joe would bring it later, but there's no telling when he'll have time."

"How about Chinese?"

"It won't take long to fix the spaghetti."

He nodded toward the sleeping child. "She might need you. It would be difficult to care for her and cook."

Maggie nearly laughed at his logic. Women had juggled babies and housework for years. She'd feel insulted if she didn't know he had good intentions. "I don't mind not cooking. Chicken and broccoli would hit the spot. Let me get some money."

"I've got it."

Maggie protested, "I don't expect you to feed me, Dillon."

"You can return the favor next time."

After he'd gone, Maggie considered the implications of there being a next time. Apparently, Dillon Rogers planned to make himself at home in her life.

Right at home. How did he do that? Dillon believed he belonged everywhere he went. She'd craved that elusive feeling since her father died.

Was it her? What kept her from accepting her right to belong? Despite the fact that her friends welcomed her into the community with open arms, there were still times when she felt like an outsider.

Maggie doubted Dillon had any idea how she felt. Nor did she feel an overwhelming need to share her lack of self-esteem.

Little Mary Margaret Gregory had once had self-esteem, before foster homes had left her drifting in the wind, as homeless as tumbleweed blowing through the desert. She hadn't fit in there, either, because she was the outsider—the child the family allowed to live in their home. Even adopted children knew they had a special place in their parents' hearts, but foster children were more like nomads.

In her foster care years, Maggie had become acquainted with more than one child in the system because their parents couldn't be bothered to accept their responsibility. Then there were the kids like her whose lives had taken a turn for the worst and left them homeless wards of the state.

Maggie understood Peg's concern about her daughter. Where would Chloe go if something happened to her mother? Back to the father who couldn't put aside his own selfish needs to care about his wife and small child? She didn't even want to consider that possibility.

Maggie pushed herself off the recliner and ran out to the car to get the bags she'd brought from Peg's home. In the kitchen, she sorted the items. No doubt, Chloe would be hungry when she woke. Maggie smiled at the worn stuffed teddy Peg reminded her Chloe couldn't be without. She remembered seeing it in the little girl's arms when she came to the nursery. Obviously, Mrs. Pearson hadn't known that when she grabbed Chloe and headed for the hospital.

They napped until well after lunch. When she woke, Maggie called Natalie to ask if she could stay with Chloe that night. She agreed and said she'd come over to get acquainted with the child before Maggie left for work.

Dillon returned midafternoon and brought their meal inside before going back to his car for the playpen and high chair. "Mari showed me how to set them up. I'll show you when she wakes up."

"Chloe," Maggie said. He looked at her strangely. "Her name is Chloe. Her mother's name is Peg."

His bewildered expression told her he didn't understand. "I'm sure Peg and Chloe appreciate your efforts on their behalf. I wanted you to know their names."

Dillon shifted uncomfortably. "Well. . . Um. . . It's the least I can do."

She found his discomfort surprising. "I appreciate your help, too. It's sweet of you."

He grinned widely. "Let's eat before our food gets cold."

Maggie checked on Chloe and returned to the kitchen. She sat down at the table and served her plate from the various containers. "I really should wake her up. She won't sleep tonight."

"Give her a few more minutes—just until you finish eating."

Maggie chose a seat where she could keep Chloe in sight. "What's the next step with the house?" she asked as she removed her egg roll from the wrapper. "If this contractor can't start until September, that's probably going to be the case with all of them."

"Let's see what Wyatt has to offer. I wouldn't have hired this man. I didn't feel good about him."

They finished, and Dillon helped Maggie set up the playpen in her bedroom and the high chair in the kitchen. Chloe woke hungry, and he entertained the baby while Maggie prepared her meal.

Afterward Chloe played on the floor at their feet as she and Dillon watched television. When Chloe started to fuss, she joined the baby on the quilts and made her laugh.

"You're good with her," Dillon commented.

"It's good experience for when I become a foster parent." He grew quiet. "Is something wrong, Dillon?"

"No. No," he denied quickly.

"You seem troubled."

"Just thinking. You want me to keep an eye on her while you get dressed for work?"

"Natalie should be here shortly. She's spending the night."

He stood up. "Call me tomorrow if you need someone to care for her so you can rest."

"Thanks, Dillon. We'll be fine. She goes to day care."

He took Maggie's hand in his and squeezed gently. "Have a good night. I'll be in touch about the house."

❧

After letting himself out Maggie's back door, Dillon headed for the gate that separated their yards. *That was close*, he realized, thinking how easily she'd picked up on his mood. She was too perceptive. He did feel troubled. Maggie's maternal behavior seemed out of place with the woman in his head.

The child's needs would preempt his opportunity to spend time with Maggie. Working on the house gave him a good excuse to visit often, but now he'd have to share Maggie with a little girl.

And what was that about becoming a foster parent? She'd never mentioned that before.

Oh, don't be so selfish, he told himself as he secured the gate and walked across his freshly mowed lawn. What had Mom always said? When something's meant to be, God works it out.

❧

After he left, Maggie concentrated on getting Chloe bathed. She felt worn out from entertaining the little girl.

The phone rang around four thirty, and she left Chloe playing on the quilt while she grabbed the cordless from the kitchen.

"Maggie, I hear someone tried to take a shortcut through your living room," Kim exclaimed.

"Welcome home," Maggie said, happy to hear from her friend. She walked back into the living room. "How was Charleston?"

"Okay, I guess. I only had eyes for Wyatt."

"Says a woman in love," Maggie teased. "He should have saved his money and kept you at home."

"No way."

"From what Dillon said, I take it Chase is eager to see Florida."

"That child is wearing me out," Kim said. "I know I'll never want to see some of these rides he's talking about again."

"They are easier on the body when you're Chase's age."

Chloe screamed, and Kim said, "I didn't realize you had company."

Maggie handed the baby her toy as she explained the situation.

"Is Peg okay?"

"She will be. I'm watching Chloe until she's back on her feet. I think I'll bring Peg here after she gets out of the hospital. Her place is too small for me to stay there, and I have the guest room and can help with Chloe until she's able to take over."

"Let me know if I can help," Kim said. "Wyatt said Dillon is looking for contractors for you."

"He's been a great help," Maggie said, unsure she wanted to explain the matter further.

"So you two are getting along?"

"I think we'll be able to get past the history. He went over to Mari's for the playpen and high chair, and he picked up lunch today. He acted like a woman my age never dealt with children or something. He'd freak if he saw me with all those kids in the nursery."

"Probably. Wyatt just called him. Hopefully, he'll find someone soon."

"I hope so. I miss my windows. And my door." At least the space was usable. The men had boarded the opening with plywood inside and out and cleaned up the debris. It might look a little rough, but she felt secure in her home.

"I know, but consider the possibilities," Kim told her. "Now you can do some of that exterior remodeling you've always thought would suit the house."

"My fountain's broken."

"Oh," Kim moaned. "Don't worry. We'll find one that's even better."

"I'll hold you to that. When do your parents leave?"

"Next weekend. We'll be back on Friday so we can spend time with them, and then the next Monday is the first day of school."

"You're going to have a busy week. Have fun with your new family."

"I will," Kim said with a laugh.

"Let's get together soon."

"I'll call you."

"Say a prayer for Chloe tonight. She misses her mommy. I hope she doesn't give Natalie a hard time."

"Already done. Take care."

six

Early Monday morning, Natalie reported that she and Chloe had a good night and took the little girl off to day care so Maggie could sleep. She picked Chloe up that afternoon, and Natalie returned to stay the night just before Maggie went to work.

On Tuesday, Maggie insisted Dillon stay for supper. He'd stopped by to discuss an estimate from the contractor he had met with Monday evening after Maggie had left for work and offered to care for Chloe while she finished their meal. Maggie laughed when Dillon showed his horror at the way Chloe smeared food from head to toe and across the high chair in her efforts to feed herself.

"Hey, we don't do that," he protested when she banged her bowl on the high chair and then tossed it on the floor. Dillon ripped off several paper towels to clean up the mess.

"You might not do it now, but you did when you were her age," Maggie told him.

"I can't imagine Mom allowing me to be that messy."

"It's learning to be independent, Dillon. How else will she learn to feed and dress herself?"

He deposited the towels in the trash. "So I should be telling her 'good job'?"

Maggie grinned and nodded. "While encouraging her to get more in her mouth than on her body, of course."

She set a bowl of rice on the table and added the beef stew she'd cooked with onions, potatoes, and carrots in the slow cooker. "Eat your dinner. I'll take over with Chloe."

He served his plate and took a bite. "This is delicious."

"Thanks. So tell me about the contractor."

He changed gears quickly, wiping his mouth as he said, "He's the one we should use. I'm impressed with his knowledge level, and he can start right away."

"Right away?" she questioned. He'd told her most of the others he'd called were backlogged for months.

Dillon reached for his iced tea and took a long drink before he nodded. "My advice is to give them the job. Unless you want to wait for more estimates."

Maggie wasn't sure. "You're comfortable with this guy?"

"Keith Harris gave me references, and they all checked out. Three satisfied customers said both he and his brother do excellent work."

"Then why is he available so soon?" Maggie asked.

"It's the craziest story. He and his twin brother, Erik, are married to sisters. Both wives were expecting, and the babies were born on the same day. They cleared their calendars to help at home. Now they're ready to start booking again and willing to make yours their first project. Answer to a prayer, wouldn't you say?"

Maggie remembered reading about the couples in the paper. "Oh yes," she agreed without further hesitation. "I'm so tired of that cave I call my living room. I need light."

"I'll call Keith right now."

"He might be busy," she said.

"He's expecting my call." Dillon unclipped his cell phone and dialed her new contractor. "He'll be here tomorrow," he told her after disconnecting.

"You were sure I'd say yes, weren't you?" Maggie asked, mildly put out by his actions.

"We need to act fast, before they get more projects in the works. Keith gave me a materials list. I placed the order this morning and picked these up while I was at the hardware store." He indicated the door and window brochures he'd laid on the tabletop earlier.

"What happened to carrying out my decisions?" she demanded.

His pleading blue gaze begged her forgiveness. "I'm sorry.

When he told me they could start tomorrow, I knew they needed supplies."

"And you couldn't pick up the phone to call and ask?"

He frowned and said, "You were sleeping. Do you want me to cancel the order?"

It annoyed her more that he tried to use charm to coax her into a better mood. "No, Dillon. Did you pay for the stuff?"

He reached for his wallet. "I have the receipt right here. You can reimburse me when you get your check from the insurance company."

Maggie didn't like being in his debt. She had planned to use her credit card. She'd known this would happen. "Fine."

"What about the door and windows? Do you have any idea what you want?"

"A few, but I'll look at the brochures tonight after I get Chloe into bed."

"We should visit a couple of stores so you can see the doors and windows before you decide."

"I'm off the rest of the week. I bring Peg home from the hospital on Friday."

Dillon finished his meal and indicated she should eat. He used paper towels to wipe Chloe's face and hands and wiped the high chair down with a sponge. "You're bringing her home?"

"She's still recovering, Dillon. She can't take care of Chloe on her own."

He grimaced when Chloe let out a loud wail of protest because he didn't take her from the high chair. "I still don't understand why you're making this your problem."

"It's not a problem. While she recovers from her surgery, Peg's not allowed to lift more than ten pounds. If she goes home alone with Chloe, she won't have a choice, and then she'll be back in the hospital. I've discussed it with Natalie and Mari, and they're willing to help."

"You don't leave anything to chance, do you?"

Maggie laid her fork on the plate and went to get Chloe

a cookie. "Rarely. It's never been an option for me. Not if I want my life to run smoothly."

"Your life would glide if you didn't take on so much."

"What would you do, Dillon?" Maggie demanded. When he said nothing, she said, "Let me answer that for you. When it's something you can handle, like finding my contractor, you're on it without hesitation. But this situation with Peg and Chloe isn't something you can handle, is it?"

He looked sheepish. "I suppose not."

"There are too many people in the world who never ask anything of their fellow man until they're knocked off their feet and forced to seek help. Do you think Peg likes giving up her independence?

"Not in the least. And she'll spend weeks trying to figure out some way to repay me. But that's not my reason for helping. I'm doing this for Chloe." Maggie ran her hand over the child's red curls. "You need me, don't you, sweetie?"

The baby laughed.

"So if it were just Peg, you wouldn't be doing this?"

She forced herself to settle down. "I'd still help, but she wouldn't need more than a few groceries, maybe a ride home from the hospital or to the doctor's office, and perhaps a bit of medical advice," she explained. "I'm a nurse. Taking care of people is what I do best."

"Another good reason not to take it on in your private life."

"We're not going to agree. Until Peg's able to care for Chloe without endangering herself, I'm helping out."

"Do you think Natalie or Mari would keep an eye on her when we go shopping?"

Maggie studied the messy baby. "We could take Chloe with us."

"To the hardware store? There are a million things she could get into."

Chloe took that moment to toss her spoon on the floor. It clattered against the tile. "That's why they put child seats on shopping carts."

Dillon looked doubtful. "Fine. What about tomorrow?"

"I think I need to be here to make sure the Harris brothers understand what I want. What about Friday afternoon? It'll probably be close to noon before I get Peg home and settled."

"What about day care?" Dillon asked. "You are planning to take Chloe, aren't you?"

Maggie had no plans to change the baby's schedule. Besides, it would be hard for her to rest with demolition and construction going on. And as for Friday, she knew Peg was eager to see her daughter, but things would be easier all around if she left Chloe at day care until later that afternoon. "I'll run it by Peg."

"Coming home is going to take a lot out of her. She can rest and then spend quality time with her child Friday night."

❧

Dillon was right. Peg was exhausted from the exertion of the trip home and agreed she needed time to get herself together before seeing Chloe. Maggie brought Peg home, fixed her lunch, and helped her into bed for a long nap. She apologized for the construction noise, but Peg assured her she didn't mind. After making sure Peg had everything she needed nearby, Maggie called Dillon.

He took her to a discount hardware store, and they looked through the various windows and doors on display. A beautiful oak door with a leaded glass panel and matching sidelights struck her fancy, and even though Maggie told herself it was more than she had planned to spend, she kept trying to work it out in her head.

"You should get it," Dillon said when she went back to examine the door for the third time.

"It costs three times as much as the others," she argued. "And if I get a cheaper door, I can have those bigger windows."

"I could look around for something similar that costs less," he offered. "Only thing is the Harrises will need them soon."

"I'm sure I can find one here," Maggie said.

"What about carpet for the living room?"

"Just a new area rug," Maggie said. Thankfully, her old rug had protected the floors from the gas, oil, and radiator fluids that had poured from the car. "I love the hardwoods. I worked hard to restore them."

He looked surprised. "You did the floors?"

She nodded. "Mrs. Allene said I could. I ripped up the old carpet and rented a sander. Once I got used to the machine, it wasn't bad." Maggie grinned and admitted, "A time or two, I thought I'd gone too deep, but thankfully I hadn't."

"What else did you do to the house?"

"Painted, replaced the bathroom vanity and kitchen counters, and tiled the kitchen floor."

"Mom let you pay for all that?"

Maggie shrugged. "Why should she pay? I rented a perfectly good house. I wanted the changes."

"But you improved her property."

The reality of the matter was that she'd improved her own property, but Maggie had no way of knowing that would be the case. She wondered if her work had been the reason Mrs. Allene left her the house.

"Did you landscape the yard, too?"

"I love to garden. That reminds me. Did the adjustor cover that in the estimate?"

"He did, but I don't think he paid what the statuary was worth."

"They were all secondhand pieces. I have the receipts. Kim found the fountain for me."

"I looked it over and think we might be able to salvage it with epoxy and concrete paint."

"Won't it leak?" Maggie asked.

"If it doesn't work, all we've lost is the cost of the supplies. If it does, you'll have your fountain back."

Maggie walked back to the oak door. "I'm going to buy this one. If I don't, I'll kick myself later when I start wishing I had. Besides, I won't need bigger windows with the glass in the door and panels."

"Good point. Today's your lucky day. Wyatt has an account with this store, and he gets a discount. He said to charge whatever we need, and we'll settle up later."

Pleased with how things were falling into place, Maggie laughed joyously. "I need to shop with you more often."

After picking out her windows and shingles for the new roof, they headed for home.

"Thanks for your help, Dillon. I didn't look forward to handling this alone."

"No problem. I'll pick up the fountain later and take it over to my workshop."

"I doubt it can be repaired, but you're welcome to give it a try."

"I like making things work when people think it's impossible."

Maggie had seen that facet of his personality in action numerous times. Maybe it was something to do with being an engineer. "Are you coming over for dinner?"

"No. I'm sure your houseguest will want to get to bed early."

"Well, thanks again," she said as she opened the car door. "I'm going to pick up Chloe. Peg's waited long enough to see her child."

Later that night, when Peg and Chloe were sleeping, Maggie found herself missing Dillon. Sure, there were times when she considered him controlling, but the good outweighed the bad.

She thought about the door they'd found that day. It was perfect. Something else she'd never considered she'd have—a home of her own with a beautiful leaded glass and oak front door to welcome her friends.

seven

On Sunday, Maggie dressed Chloe for church and then took her in to say good-bye to her mother.

"Wish I were going," Peg said as she righted Chloe's hair bow. The baby's hand immediately went to her head.

Maggie knew how Peg felt. She didn't have her strength back, but she was tired of being a convalescent. They had become better acquainted since Peg had moved in. Last night, after Chloe was in bed, they sat and chatted until time for bed.

"Is Peg short for Peggy?" Maggie asked.

"No. Mary Margaret."

Maggie smiled. "I'm Mary Margaret, too."

"Your mom's best friend?" Peg asked.

"Grandmothers," Maggie offered. "Both died before I had an opportunity to know them."

"It's old-fashioned," Peg said. "I wanted Chloe to have something unique. Of course, now that I think about it, there will be hundreds of Chloes and only a few Mary Margarets."

Peg thanked Maggie for stepping in to care for her daughter. Maggie understood Peg's concerns and felt thankful for the opportunity to be of service to someone in need.

"No, Chloe," Peg said, bringing Maggie's thoughts back to the present.

Maggie tried to clip the hair bow back in place and gave up when Chloe wouldn't leave it alone. "We'd better go."

She told Chloe to tell Mommy good-bye and smiled when the child worked her fingers in response. Grabbing the stroller from the laundry room, they went outside and saw Dillon coming out his back door.

It was a gorgeous day, the sun shining brightly and not a

cloud in the sky. No doubt the beach was already filled with sun worshippers. Maggie sent up a quick prayer for them as she struggled to keep her hold on Chloe while opening the stroller.

"Good morning, ladies," Dillon said, coming over to complete the task for her. "It's a beautiful day for service to the Lord."

"I'm putting Chloe in the nursery and attending worship service today."

"Want to sit with me?"

"I'll meet you in the sanctuary after Sunday school."

As Maggie went off toward the nursery, Dillon headed to the room where his Sunday school group met. He enjoyed being in fellowship with men his own age. His worship in Saudi Arabia had been much different.

One of the things Dillon appreciated most was the freedom to worship. It might have been something he took for granted in the past, but having lived in a Muslim country for so many years, he found himself very appreciative of Cornerstone.

After greeting the others, he took a seat and allowed his thoughts to drift back to Maggie in her caregiver mode. She seemed so comfortable with Chloe.

Maybe it was because she was a nurse, but no matter how he tried, Dillon couldn't help but feel Maggie allowed people to take advantage of her. Awareness washed over him like waves washing up on shore. No wonder he'd hurt her with his insinuations. Now that he knew her better, he realized she wasn't capable of what he had implied.

The class began, and soon it was time to meet Maggie. They sat in his parents' pew. Having her by his side was nice. When they sang, he enjoyed her alto voice. When Joe Dennis invited them to read along in their Bibles, she shared.

"No doubt some of you in here today are carrying a load of guilt over past sins," Pastor Joe began. "Something you can't let go of even though your heavenly Father has removed this sin to the depths of the ocean.

"And we all know that ocean is pretty deep. You can't dive to the bottom without oxygen, and even then you can only stay down a brief time. Forgiven sin isn't like that. It doesn't bob to the surface when we least expect it. Once you've repented and been forgiven, that sin no longer exists in God's eyes.

"Oh, we hold on to it," Joe Dennis pronounced gravely. "Maybe as penance for our wicked ways. Self-punishment to keep us from forgetting. Or maybe we hold on to remind ourselves we're not worthy of Jesus Christ dying for our sins. But friends, we are worthy indeed. Christ made us worthy.

"Now listen carefully. I'm not saying we should ever take the gift for granted. We should embrace His love with open arms and freely offer it to anyone with ears to listen."

As the sermon continued, Dillon's discomfort increased. He glanced at Maggie to find her listening to the pastor's words, nodding in agreement.

"If there's a burden on your heart today because you need to seek forgiveness from someone, then you should pray and take action to resolve the situation immediately. Only then can you walk with God as He would have you walk."

Each word stabbed Dillon in the heart. He was a Christian. He had given his heart to Jesus as a child of seven, but he still had to fight the ways of the world. And he definitely needed to seek forgiveness of someone he'd hurt by his actions.

When Maggie decided not to stay for fellowship and collected Chloe from the nursery, Dillon joined her for the walk home.

"Can we talk for a few minutes?"

She seemed eager to escape. "I'm sure Peg is ready for lunch."

"Just a few minutes, Maggie. Please," Dillon pleaded. "Chloe is happy right now, and I'm sure Peg can wait that long."

"Not today. Not now."

"Why?" he asked. "I'm trying to say I'm sorry. Is it too much for you to accept my apology?"

"Yes," Maggie said. "There's nothing to forgive."

"You know there is," Dillon insisted with a stubbornness reminiscent of his mother.

"What I know is that Mrs. Allene was your mother, not mine. You should have doubts about me," Maggie said, stooping to pick up the toy Chloe tossed from the stroller.

Dillon bent at the same time, and they butted heads. "Why are you saying this, Maggie?" he asked as he straightened up, rubbing his skull.

"Because I heard that sermon today, too, Dillon. I haven't been able to see my role in our problems because of the beam in my own eye."

Dillon shook his head and insisted, "I was wrong. Now that I know you better, I know you'd never willingly take advantage of another living soul. I misjudged you, and I'm sorry."

"You don't understand."

Confusion drove him to ask, "Understand what?"

"It's stupid, but I felt I no longer belonged."

"Belonged where?"

"Here," Maggie explained. "In your mother's life. In my hometown."

"But how could you feel that way? You're a member of the community. A member of Cornerstone. People love you."

"But I took something that wasn't mine to take."

"How do you figure that?"

"You'd have to understand my past," she said, looking everywhere but at Dillon.

He lifted her chin and gazed into her eyes. "Tell me."

"You remember I was a foster child?" Dillon nodded, and she continued. "I became a loner. Being a foster child does that to you. You wander in and out of people's lives, like going through a revolving door.

"My problem was I tried too hard. Whenever the parents said 'why can't you be more like Maggie?' I saw the writing on the wall. A good foster kid learns to fly under the radar, but I wanted to be loved. I thought being good would help.

But I was wrong."

"But surely the parents knew it wasn't your fault if their children were jealous."

"It didn't matter," Maggie declared. "The foster parents weren't going to make their lives miserable. Oh, some of them showed regret. After all, I was an easy foster child. I did more than my fair share of chores and made good grades in school."

"What about your last foster parents? Did they make you feel that way?"

"The Floyds are good people," Maggie said. "But my insecurities were well established by that time. I'd been in the system for years, and I didn't dare get too comfortable for fear I'd get sent away again."

"But it didn't happen."

"No, but I lived daily with the knowledge that it could. You grew up and made the decision to leave home, Dillon. I had no home to leave. You can't begin to imagine what it's like to be forced to depend on the kindness and mercy of strangers."

"Like Peg?" he asked with a dawning understanding.

Maggie nodded. "My needs have always been pretty basic. I have to feel people love and want me in their lives."

"And I made you feel you don't belong?" he repeated.

"No, not you. Me," Maggie stated, resting her hands against her chest to emphasize her point. "When you questioned my intentions, I went on the defensive because I felt this sense of entitlement about Mrs. Allene. I became that little girl who wanted to be someone's daughter. Your mother's daughter."

"There's nothing wrong with that," Dillon said. "My mother loved you and rightfully so, because truth be told, you were a better daughter than I was a son. I knew she wasn't going to live forever. I just didn't know how little time I had."

"None of us do, Dillon. That's why it's important to tell people you love them at every opportunity. I felt envy when she talked about you. I sound like a candidate for a psychologist's couch."

"Not really. Sometimes when we can't have what we want

in life, we reach out and take. You wanted a mother, and I had one I took for granted."

"She was a wonderful woman."

"I'm glad we can share our memories of her," Dillon said.

"So where do we stand?"

"I consider you a good friend, Maggie, but I feel the need to explore another depth to our relationship. I care for you."

What is she thinking? Dillon wondered, watching her expression as she considered what he'd just shared with her.

Chloe started to fuss, and Maggie glanced down at the child. "I'd better get her home."

"Maggie?" Dillon said as she pushed the stroller forward a couple of steps. "You won't let what I just told you scare you off, will you?"

She glanced back at him. "No, Dillon. If God has something more in store for us, I'll be around to learn what it is."

He smiled broadly.

"I'm glad we talked. I'll have to thank Pastor Joe for his sermon."

"There's so much we don't know about each other," Maggie warned.

"There's time."

They shared another smile. Maggie invited him to lunch, and Dillon quickly accepted, eager to spend more time with her now that she'd given him a glimpse of the real Maggie Gregory.

eight

Her return to day shift and the ongoing work on the house presented Maggie with a new dilemma. She knew Peg couldn't rest comfortably with all the noise and activity. Peg suggested she could go home, but Maggie knew she couldn't care for Chloe alone yet.

Natalie solved the problem by offering to take Chloe to day care and Peg back to her apartment for the day. Mari would pick up Chloe from day care before they closed, and then Maggie would pick up Peg and Chloe after work and bring them back to her house for the night.

Maggie let Natalie in the next morning and left Chloe in her care while she showered and dressed for work. She found them in the kitchen.

"You don't have to be here so early. I don't think they plan to start work until around eight."

"I wasn't sure," Natalie said as she fed Chloe fruit. The baby smiled shyly. "She's such a sweetie."

Maggie noted Chloe's hair had been brushed up into little pigtails on each side of her head. "How did you manage that? She won't leave her bows alone."

"I sidetracked her with food. I'm sure she'll catch on shortly."

Chloe offered her own baby-speak greeting when Maggie spoke to her before pouring coffee into her travel mug. "How's Peg this morning?"

"Good. She said the pain isn't as bad. Didn't want any pills when I took her breakfast a few minutes ago."

She yawned widely. "Thanks, Nat. See you tonight."

❧

Maggie took Peg for her post-op appointment on Friday.

The doctor released her to return to work but cautioned her about overdoing.

"Are you sure you can care for Chloe?" Maggie asked when Peg announced her plans to return home.

They stopped by the church day care, and Peg watched as Maggie secured Chloe in the car seat. "You've done enough. It's time we gave you your house back."

"I haven't minded having you there."

"I know, but I'm feeling stronger every day. You gave me time to recuperate, and I thank you for that. If it hadn't been for you and Natalie, I would have had no choice but to care for Chloe myself."

"When do you want to go?"

"Today. I have everything packed."

Maggie felt tears well in her eyes. "I'm gonna miss you both so much."

"We'll miss you, too. I hope we can stay in touch," Peg offered uncertainly.

"You're not getting rid of me that easily," Maggie said with a grin. "I consider you a friend. Besides, your daughter has taken control of a chunk of my heart."

"Oh, Maggie, I can never thank you enough for all you've done."

"Seeing you well and happy is all the thanks I need," Maggie said.

Back at the house, Maggie insisted Peg rest while she loaded the car. "What about food?"

"I need a few things."

"I'll take you to your place. You can make a list, and I'll do the shopping." When Peg started to protest, Maggie held up her hand and said, "Last time, I promise."

"Okay, but you have to let us do something for you."

"Just get better."

Three hours later, Peg and Chloe had settled in at home. Maggie had restocked the kitchen, and Mrs. Pearson promised to check in on them regularly.

Overwhelming sadness filled Maggie as she walked outside and climbed into her car. She'd known she'd miss Peg and Chloe but not how much.

A public service announcement about foster parenting played on the radio, reminding Maggie to follow up on the application she'd made back in the spring. The four- to six-month review period had passed, but the accident had put things on hold. She hoped she would soon have the house repaired and get a placement.

She still couldn't believe the idea had never occurred to her until recently. And now she anticipated the prospect of sharing her home again.

Maggie parked and walked over to talk with Keith Harris for a few minutes before going inside to load the dishes into the dishwasher. Maggie smiled when she found Chloe's dish. It would give her a reason to visit sooner. She turned off the faucet after rinsing the last plate and grabbed a towel to dry her hands before answering the knock at the back door. "Dillon? What's wrong?"

She touched his arm and noted the pale dampness of his skin.

"Pain in my side. Nausea after I eat."

She took his arm and guided him toward a chair. "Why didn't you say something before?"

"Men don't whine."

Maggie grinned at that. "Suffering in silence doesn't make sense. How is the pain on a scale of one to ten?"

"A thirteen," he said, grimacing as he spoke.

"Let me grab my purse. I'll take you to the ER." She knew he was sick when he didn't argue.

An hour later, she sat by his bed in the small cubicle. The diagnosis was pancreatitis caused by gallstones.

"For now, we'll admit you in the hospital and restrict all food and water until we get this under control," the doctor said. "I'm ordering a GI cocktail. That should help some. We'll give you medication for the pain, and I'd like to do a CAT scan. Then we can look at options to eliminate the problem."

"Whatever you need to do," Dillon told them, all the while struggling to keep a stiff upper lip.

Maggie patted his hand. "You'll feel better soon."

"All that big talk about others taking advantage, and now I'm doing the same thing," he mumbled.

"It's not taking advantage if I do something willingly," Maggie said.

"I'm so thirsty," Dillon moaned.

"I'll bring you a few ice chips. Be careful though. We don't want to make things worse."

Dillon lay back against the bed. "I don't ever recall being this sick."

Maggie smoothed her hand over his forehead, and upon realizing what she'd done, jerked her hand away. That certainly wasn't very professional. "Rest for a bit."

He reached for her hand and kissed it, whispering his thanks just before he dozed off.

Maggie hated seeing Dillon like this. She prayed for him throughout her shift and had the church members doing the same. Joe and Noah came to visit, as well as Wyatt and Kim Alexander. The members of Cornerstone filled his room with flowers, cards, and balloons. By Sunday, he seemed to be doing better when she stopped in to check on him.

"I'm sorry, Maggie. I let you down."

"Don't be ridiculous, Dillon. You couldn't know you'd get sick. Besides, the Harris brothers are doing an excellent job. They got the porch roof back on and promised me a working door and new windows by next week."

"They work fast."

"They've had plenty of men checking up on them. Wyatt, Joe, and Noah drop by every day."

"All of them?"

"Well, I suspect Joe and Noah started out by witnessing, but now that they've learned the Harrises attend church, they're inspecting their work."

He managed a weak smile.

≈

On Sunday, Dillon woke feeling much better. The surgeon did his rounds early that morning.

"We can proceed with surgery or wait until a later date."

"I don't want to risk a recurrence of what just happened. Let's get this over with."

"I'll check on an operating room. Maybe this afternoon but probably tomorrow."

Dillon went to surgery, and by Monday night, Maggie was encouraging him to walk. She told him the sooner he became mobile, the sooner he'd get to go home. He managed to make it around the floor a couple of times.

"Hey, Maggie," one of the aides called, "I see you got more flowers."

She looked up just as he walked by. Dillon noted the large bouquet in the nursing station.

Who could be sending Maggie flowers? Dillon wondered as he continued his shuffle down the hall. He'd never seen any other man at her home. But no doubt she had her share of men who appreciated her beauty and personality, including him. Of course, his feelings went beyond appreciation.

In all the times he'd been in Maggie's home, he'd never seen flowers. Most women would take such a large, extravagant bouquet home to enjoy, wouldn't they?

Whatever the case, maybe it was time he sent some flowers of his own. Just to let her know he'd been serious when he'd talked about advancing their relationship.

When the doctor released him the next day, Dillon was glad to leave the confines of the hospital. When Wyatt offered to pick him up, Dillon accepted. He might be sore and stiff, but he was sick of the hospital. Well, most of it. Having Maggie as his caregiver had been a plus.

Of course, being a convalescent at home when you couldn't do anything wasn't much fun either. When the nurse reviewed his release orders with him and warned him not to lift more than ten pounds, he thought about Peg and Chloe. Funny how being in the same predicament put the situation in a completely different light.

Restless, Dillon read the paper and his e-mail and finally decided to walk over and look at Maggie's house. The Harris brothers were well on their way to completion of the job.

Keith Harris came outside and spotted Dillon. "How are you feeling?"

"Much better. It was rough going there for a while."

"I can imagine. Maggie asked us to keep you in our prayers."

"Believe me, I appreciated every prayer sent up on my behalf." He pointed at the house. "Looks good. I'm sure Maggie will be glad to have her door and windows in."

The contractor chuckled. "She's mentioned it a time or two. She'll probably do a victory dance when she opens the door the first time."

Dillon could see her doing exactly that. "Be sure to put me on your reference list."

"Business is starting to pick up again now that word is getting around, but we appreciate the referrals. The pastor stuck our card on the bulletin board over at the church."

"I appreciate the great job you've done for Maggie." The twinges of discomfort warned Dillon he'd done too much. "I'd better head on home. This surgery makes me feel like an old man."

Maggie had been called in to work extra shifts but checked on Dillon when she got home on Wednesday and Thursday. On Thursday afternoon, he remembered his plan and placed a floral order. He suspected she would have preferred going to the nursery for rosebushes but decided this would work for now.

The next morning, he watched through the window and smiled at the sight of her carrying the roses into the house. At least she hadn't given them away.

A few minutes later, he saw Maggie crossing the yard. She

tapped on the door, and he invited her in.

She smiled at him. "Good morning. How are you feeling?"

"Better."

"Did you eat?"

"Toast and coffee."

"Well, go easy on the food for a few days. You might find yourself unable to eat things you used to eat."

Dillon nodded. "How was work?"

"Good. Thanks for the flowers. They're gorgeous, but you shouldn't have."

"They were the least I could do after all you've done for me and my mom."

"I told you, Dillon, I did what I did for Mrs. Allene out of love."

"And me?"

Maggie blushed as she said, "There's a certain degree of affection involved."

"The flowers are my way of saying thank you to the beautiful woman I care for a great deal."

"Thanks. You want to come over for a late celebratory lunch after I wake this afternoon? Keith left the bill on the kitchen counter. Everything is officially back where it belongs."

Maggie's pleasure radiated out through her smile. "I should send you flowers. I owe you a great deal of thanks. You helped make a major inconvenience much easier."

"The Harris brothers did the hard work," Dillon said. "I just wandered around making comments and asking questions."

"I know you did more than that," Maggie told him.

"You want me to take care of lunch? I could order pizza or something."

"No pizza for you. I picked up a roasted chicken at the grocery store yesterday. Or I have sandwich fixings if you prefer."

"Call me when you wake up."

≈

As Maggie got into bed, her gaze drifted to the arrangement on the nightstand. She smiled as she recalled Dillon's "beautiful woman he cared for" compliment.

Sleep didn't come easily as she considered the changes in her life. She didn't feel as sad as she had after Mrs. Allene's death. Maybe because she had Dillon to occupy her time?

All she knew was that he was his mother's son. He had inherited many of the traits she'd admired in her friend. "You'd be proud, Mrs. Allene," she whispered, wishing the woman was around so she could tell her what a wonderful son she had.

After a while, exhaustion won out, and her eyes drifted shut. It was after two o'clock p.m. when she woke, and Maggie took a quick shower and washed her hair before she called Dillon. After she spoke to him, she reheated leftover green beans to go along with the chicken and potato salad. She poured glasses of lemonade just as he made an appearance.

"You want to eat in the kitchen or on the patio?"

"Let's sit outside," Dillon said. "It's a nice day. I never imagined I'd spend Labor Day in the hospital. What did you do?"

"Kim and Wyatt invited everyone to their place for an afternoon cookout."

"I can hardly believe the summer is over."

"The town was full of tourists for the holiday weekend."

"One final hurrah?"

"Some will come as long as there are sunny days," Maggie said, "but Labor Day generally marks the end of the season."

After appeasing their hunger, the conversation drifted from subject to subject.

"You lived in DC.?" Dillon asked as she talked about the Floyds.

"Just outside in Virginia. Mr. Floyd worked at the Pentagon. Tell me about Saudi Arabia. What did you do in your free time?"

"Camped, scuba dived in the Red Sea, and followed softball tournaments. They were very popular. I went to the souk often."

"The what?"

"Souk. The market. You should see the gold souks. Walls

covered in gold. They keep thievery to a minimum by chopping off the right hand."

"Sounds cruel," Maggie said.

"It's a different culture," Dillon told her. "Women don't have freedoms like here in the States. But they are a very family-focused country."

"Tell me more about the souks."

"They had some great handwoven baskets. And Persian rugs."

"Like your mom's?"

Dillon nodded. "I shipped them home to her. I have more at my place. I want to show you the ornate camel saddle I have. I really need to check into having my things sent home."

"Mrs. Allene often mentioned your letters. She loved those packages you sent."

Maggie shared a story about his mother, and Dillon seemed eager to hear more.

"I shouldn't have let time get away from me like I did."

His regret-filled words struck a chord in Maggie. She remembered her own judgmental comments but accepted that life had gotten in the way. He'd lived thousands of miles away and used the telephone as his contact.

"She would want you to look ahead, Dillon. Not back. I'm sure she told you that many times."

"Too many," he agreed. "Thanks for taking care of her."

"We took care of each other. She was a good friend."

He didn't say anything, only nodded, and Maggie saw the sheen in his eyes. Dillon still grieved his mother as she did her friend. She reached over and touched his hand gently.

"We were both very blessed to have her in our lives, and we will see her again one day."

"Another blessing," Dillon agreed. "So what are your plans now that the house is finished?"

"I'm going to put my home back together and notify foster care."

"About what?" he asked.

"I told you about my plans to become a foster parent."

"How are you going to manage that? Won't working alternating shifts every week make it impossible?"

"A number of mothers work alternating shifts at the hospital, Dillon."

"Yes, but they have husbands to help take care of the children."

"Not all of them. There are more single moms than you realize," Maggie said, adding, "but they do have family to help. I have it worked out. Once I get a placement, I'll request a day-shift schedule. Mari's agreed to help out when I have to work."

"A child is a big responsibility."

"I know that," Maggie said, finding herself a bit put out by his comment. "Believe me, I prayed over this when the idea presented itself. It's the right thing to do. There are kids who need love in their lives, and whether I provide that love for days or months, it's something I need to do."

"You need to think about what you're taking on," he argued.

"Why would you assume I haven't?"

"I didn't say that."

"You implied I hadn't. You did the same thing when I brought Chloe and Peg home."

"I offered my opinion as your friend. I'm sorry if that bothers you."

His huffy response troubled Maggie. "As my friend, you should know I do consider how my decisions affect my life."

"I'm sorry. I shouldn't have said anything."

"I'm sorry, too. It was a major decision, but it's time I gave back."

Resigned, Dillon asked, "How can I help?"

"Pray for me."

Maggie continued to make certain that Dillon didn't overdo. On her next day off, she made a dish of his mother's macaroni and cheese casserole recipe and took it over to him.

She found him sorting through old pictures at the kitchen table. After placing the casserole in the oven, Maggie walked over and picked up a photo of what appeared to be him at around age five.

"Thinking of taking up scrapbooking?" she teased.

"Strolling down memory lane. I ran across these boxes and thought I'd see if I recognized anyone."

"Have you?"

Dillon nodded. "These appear to be the family photos. Mom and Dad, me. Grandparents, aunts, uncles, cousins."

Maggie pulled out a chair and sat down. "I love old family photos. I suppose ours got dumped in the trash with the rest of our things after Daddy died."

"I'm sorry, Maggie. I wish I could give them back."

She smiled. "I'll be happy to share yours." Maggie felt herself grow warm at the implication of her words. "I mean. . . Well, I love old photos."

Dillon chuckled and pushed the box over. "Help yourself. There's at least five or six generations of old here."

She playfully tapped him on the arm and reached for a photo of a young couple, the man dressed in uniform. "Your parents?"

He nodded. "Mom always said Dad was the most handsome man she knew."

Maggie disagreed. She considered Dillon better-looking.

They sorted through photos for half an hour before the timer went off and Dillon said, "Mac and cheese time."

Maggie filled plates, and Dillon poured tea. They abandoned the photo-strewn table in favor of the island.

"Your mom has lots of pictures."

"Mom had too much junk. I've donated bins of clothes and whatnots to charity."

Maggie hated to consider what he'd given away. "Some of those whatnots were probably valuable."

Crinkles of confusion formed about his eyes as Dillon asked, "Like what?"

"Since I don't know what you donated, I can't be sure, but she collected Fenton glass and was always saying she needed more display space."

He grimaced. "I guess someone will find a real bargain at the resale shop."

His cavalier response astonished Maggie. "You don't feel any attachment? These things belonged to your mother."

"I'm not the sentimental type," Dillon declared. "I don't care for clutter. You wouldn't believe some of the stuff I've run across. This morning I found bundles of letters Dad sent Mom when they dated. And the cards I sent for birthdays and Mother's Day."

Maggie gasped. "Please tell me you didn't throw them away."

He shrugged. "Not yet. But why not?"

"It's your family history, Dillon. Your parents' love story. Don't you want to read the letters?"

"Not particularly. They're private correspondence."

"They're a treasure. A written testimony of your parents' love for one another," Maggie argued. "I don't have any of that from my parents."

"While I have an overabundance I could care less about?"

This isn't my concern, Maggie thought. But words of advice tumbled from her lips. "You don't have to keep everything, but be careful not to dispose of things you can't replace."

"I have Dad's tools. And I kept their books. I'm going to build shelving around the fireplace in the family room to hold them all."

"Some of your mom's knickknacks would look good on those shelves," Maggie suggested. "And if you're so determined to get rid of stuff, at least talk with Kim. She'll give you a fair deal."

Dillon eyed her for a moment. "You think I'm heartless, don't you?"

Maggie knew it was unfair to judge others based on her own situation. Maybe if she had several lifetimes of possessions to choose from, she'd feel the need to give up things, as well.

"No," Maggie said. "I just hope you kept a list for tax purposes."

"It wasn't worth the trouble."

Maggie had never known anyone who didn't need tax write-offs.

"How do I know what to keep?" Dillon asked, sounding somewhat dismayed by the idea.

"Surely you have favorites."

"A few. What do I do with the rest?"

"No one in the family wants anything?"

"My cousin wanted a quilt our grandmother made for Mom."

Maggie recalled the beautiful quilt that his mother had treasured. She felt sad that he hadn't held on to it for his mother's sake. "She loved that quilt."

"Leslie wants to give it to her daughter," Dillon said. "At least that way something gets passed on to another generation."

"That's a true negative of being single," Maggie admitted. "Of course, most kids today don't want their parents' junk, either." She covered her mouth. "I'm sorry. I didn't mean that as a criticism."

"I know. I doubt Mom was so attached to her things that she'd want me holding on to stuff I don't want. I promise not to dispose of anything else without asking first."

"You don't need to ask me," Maggie said hastily.

"But you know what was important to Mom."

"It needs to have special meaning for you, Dillon."

"You can tell me about the truly special pieces. I've been meaning to ask if you wanted any of her jewelry."

Maggie thought about the valuable pieces Mrs. Allene had worn over the years. Particularly the string of pearls Maggie adored. "Keep the jewelry, Dillon. You might want it for your wife one day."

"And supposing there's no future Mrs. Rogers?"

"At least hang on to it for a couple of years before you decide," Maggie suggested. "You could share some of her costume pieces with the elderly ladies at church. Just sort out the expensive stuff first."

"I think most of that might be in the wall safe," Dillon said. "Though I've yet to find the combination."

Maggie recalled the time Mrs. Allene had the safe lock drilled. She'd asked Maggie to help her remember the combination. "Seems like she told me she'd used her anniversary and your birthday. I don't know the order or anything. She said the hint would jog her memory if she forgot again."

Dillon grabbed a pad and scribbled the information. "I'll give it a try. The attic is bursting at the seams, too," Dillon told her. "Some stuff has to go. I promise to be more selective in my disposal, but they're only things. Nothing here brings back the good memories of my parents. They're right here," he added, tapping his temple lightly.

Maggie considered her lack of good memories. There were a few with her dad, but they seemed so distant now.

"That's because you've always known exactly where home was. It seems like I've searched my entire life for the place that made me feel that way. South Carolina is as close as I've come."

"Until I came back and made you feel as if you'd done something wrong?"

Maggie avoided his gaze. "I never had an ulterior motive except maybe to experience some of that magnanimous love Mrs. Allene heaped on everyone."

He smiled regretfully. "I'm sorry. I never meant to hurt you. You know all your friends don't hesitate to rush to your defense. I felt like a jerk when Julie told me I should be ashamed for thinking negative thoughts about you. Mari backed her up."

"They told me," Maggie admitted. "I never asked them to talk to you."

He grinned at her. "We may be getting to know each other, but that's one thing I already know about you. You fight your own battles."

"I have been known to run away from a few," she countered.

Dillon tipped her chin and kissed her gently. "That's okay, too, just as long as you don't run away from us."

nine

As September moved forward, Maggie appreciated their growing friendship even more. She and Dillon spent a lot of time together—at church, dining out, even taking long walks along the beach. It seemed only natural that he would be on the list of people she called to share her news.

"I'm getting a foster child today. A short-term placement. Her name is Marsha Kemp, and she's ten."

"When does she arrive?"

"After school. I have to run. There's so much to do before she gets here. I need to buy groceries and get her a welcome present."

"Slow down, or you'll burn yourself out before she gets there."

Maggie laughed and said, "Talk to you later."

After three that afternoon, Maggie heard a car door slam, and it was all she could do not to meet the caseworker in the driveway. She opened the door, smiling widely as she viewed the child who had come to stay with her. Preteen and rail thin with long dark hair and a doubt-filled expression summarized her best.

The caseworker introduced them. "Marsha Kemp, this is Maggie Gregory."

Maggie held out her hand, and the child offered hers in return. "Welcome, Marsha. Let me show you where you'll be staying."

She led the way down the hall to her converted guest room. Maggie had packed away her things and splurged on a few items she thought Marsha might enjoy. When Maggie talked about painting the room in colors that would appeal to children, Dillon had helped. The room sported aqua and purple walls that matched the new striped bedspread and drapes. "Come into the living room after you unpack, and we'll get to know each other."

The girl nodded, appearing quiet and withdrawn.

"God, help me deal with this," Maggie prayed softly as she followed Mrs. Prince back into the living room.

"This is Marsha's first time away from home," the caseworker said. "Her mother got involved with the wrong man and has been incarcerated for thirty days."

"I'll do everything possible to help her."

"I know you will. Don't hesitate to call with any question." The woman handed her a business card. "We appreciate your willingness to help."

After Mrs. Prince left, Maggie waited in the living room, glancing repeatedly at the clock. What was taking so long? The phone rang, and she reached for the cordless she'd left on the arm of the sofa earlier.

"Hi. How's it going with your foster child?" Dillon asked.

"She's unpacking."

"I thought maybe we could order pizza later."

"It's better if it's just me and her tonight. It's tough on her, Dillon."

"Yeah, I can imagine. How about you ladies let me take you out this weekend?"

"I'll see what Marsha thinks and let you know."

"You will let me spend time with you, won't you?"

She heard Marsha coming down the hallway. "Gotta go. Talk to you later."

Maggie smiled at the child, noting her red-rimmed eyes. "How's your room?" Marsha shrugged. "Anything you need?"

Marsha's head barely moved in response.

"What's your favorite food?"

Marsha shrugged, her gaze fixed on the floor.

"Come on," Maggie urged. "There's something you really like. How about pizza? I like everything on mine."

"Cheese."

Maggie felt as though she'd received a gift in the one word. "How about a half and half for dinner tonight?"

Marsha nodded.

"Are you hungry? Or would you like to visit for a while?" Even as she asked, Maggie could see the child was hungry but afraid to say so. "Let's order now. I have soda, and I think we have chips. We can have a few while we wait. Let me show you the kitchen."

Maggie held the phone between her head and shoulder as she placed the order and poured soda for Marsha and iced tea for herself. She dumped a few chips into a small bowl and carried it over to the table. "Pizza will be here in twenty minutes. So you want to tell me about you, or should I go first?"

Marsha pushed a chip into her mouth and pointed at Maggie.

"I'm Mary Margaret Gregory. Everyone calls me Maggie. I'm single, and I don't have any children. I'm a nurse and work at the hospital. I go to church at Cornerstone Community Church and have some really great friends. Do you go to church?"

Maggie's heart wrenched when the child's head moved from side to side. "My pastor and his wife have five kids. They're younger than you, but I'd like you to meet them. My friend Kim and her husband, Wyatt, have a son named Chase. He's twelve. There's also Julie and Noah. He's the associate pastor at the church. And my friend Natalie. Dillon, he's my neighbor and a good friend. He'd like to meet you, too," she said, the words rushing out in a nervous gush. "You're ten?" The child nodded. "When's your birthday?"

"October twenty-fifth."

Maggie made a note of the date. Marsha would still be with her. Maybe the idea of planning something special would help the child settle in. "I'm scared, too, Marsha. You're my first foster child. I know you miss your mom, but I'd like to be your friend."

The doorbell rang. "There's our pizza."

Back in the kitchen, Maggie took paper plates and napkins from the cabinet and refilled their glasses. She set the pizza box on the table.

"Let's say grace," Maggie said, holding out her hand. After a few moments' pause, Marsha laid her hand in hers. Maggie thanked Jesus for their food and for Marsha. When she pushed the open box in the child's direction, she took one slice.

Maggie slid two onto her plate and encouraged Marsha to eat. The room grew quiet. "Since neither of us knows what to expect, how about we set some ground rules. I know I'm a stranger, but I want to be a good parent. That means I do the things your real mom does. I have to be sure you eat and get your rest and do your homework."

"Why did they make her go away?" the child asked, tears trailing down her cheeks.

"Sometimes adults make bad choices," Maggie explained as she drew the girl into her arms and rocked back and forth. "Your mom didn't want to leave you, but she had to for a while. I'll take good care of you, Marsha. I promise. Will you let me?"

The child nodded.

"Let's finish our dinner. Did you decide what you're wearing to school tomorrow?"

Marsha shook her head.

"How about I help you choose something after dinner?"

"Okay."

Maggie felt as if she'd hurtled over a high jump. And tonight was just the beginning.

Later, after Marsha had gone to sleep, Maggie reached for the phone and called Mari.

"How did it go?"

"She doesn't understand why they took her mom away."

"Poor kid. Life is such a struggle without being removed from your loved ones."

"Tell me about it."

"Do you think your experience as a foster child will help?"

"I never really understood why my parents had to die, but I survived. Marsha will, too. At least her mom is coming back for her."

"Hopefully a wiser woman," Mari said. "I'd hate to see Marsha end up in the system when she could be with her mom."

"But I'd rather she stayed there than have this happen over and over again," Maggie said.

"We'll pray for her and her mother," Mari promised.

"Her birthday is in October. She's turning eleven. I thought maybe I could plan something for her."

"That's a good idea. Planning a party will take her mind off things."

"I need to figure out what girls her age like."

"Are you allowed to give her gifts?"

"Yes. We're encouraged to celebrate events. I told her about my friends. And about church. She doesn't attend."

"Maybe another reason God placed her in your life."

Maggie considered Mari's words. When she'd prayed about becoming a foster parent, it had been to help a child who needed a parent. She hadn't considered the possibility that the child would need her heavenly Father.

"Could be. I'd better get to bed. I have to take her to school in the morning."

"Did you get your shift change?"

"They're working on it. I arranged for the church day care to pick her up from school."

"And I'll pick her up from the church on the days you work and bring her here."

Maggie had approached Mari with the plan back when she first started to think about foster parenting. "I talked with my supervisor today, and she's going to arrange for me to get off early this week. If it's okay, I thought I'd bring her by tomorrow night."

"Come for dinner."

"Okay. Night, Mari."

Maggie looked in on Marsha and found her asleep, hugging a worn Raggedy Ann doll. She adjusted the covers and turned on a night-light in the bathroom before going to her own room.

She woke early the next morning, her thoughts filled with getting Marsha to school on time. In the kitchen, Maggie considered the possibilities for breakfast.

After everything was prepared, she knocked on Marsha's door. The child was nearly dressed. "I fixed grits and eggs for breakfast. That okay?"

Marsha nodded.

Back in the kitchen, Maggie placed a package in the chair. Marsha looked at it in surprise.

Maggie had chosen the book bag and accessories after making sure Marsha didn't already have one. "It's for you."

They developed a routine. The first day, Maggie took Marsha to and from school. That night, she introduced her to the Dennis family. Marsha immediately bonded with the children. The first time she laughed at Luke and their cat, Maggie knew everything would be okay.

On her first Sunday, Maggie took Marsha to church. She knew it would be yet another new experience, but she showed the child her Sunday school classroom and depended on Julie to make Marsha comfortable. Afterward, Julie mentioned how well Chase and Marsha had gotten along.

That afternoon they went to visit Peg and Chloe. Marsha's fascination with Chloe was obvious. They played together as Peg and Maggie talked.

"She'll make a good babysitter," Peg said as she observed Marsha's gentle ways with her daughter. The child responded softly to the baby as they rolled a musical ball back and forth.

Maggie was glad to hear Peg had no problems since her return to her florist job. "Is there anything you need? I mean. . . Well, being out of work is difficult."

"We're fine. Besides, I should be asking that question," Peg said. "I can't tell you how much I appreciate all you've done. You're a wonderful friend."

"I didn't do a thing you wouldn't have done if the roles had been reversed."

"I just hope you remember that when my time comes."

"It doesn't have to be for me. Just pass it on. Help someone who needs help." Maggie glanced at her watch. "We need to be going soon. Dillon's taking us to dinner."

"How is he?"

"Much better. He understands how you felt."

"Most men can't stand being sick."

Maggie knew Peg was thinking of her husband, and her heart went out to the woman. It must hurt her badly to have her husband walk away like that.

⁂

Dillon took Maggie and Marsha to a popular cafeteria. They chose foods and placed them on their trays, carrying them into the large dining room. They chose a table and emptied their trays. "I have to go to Columbia. Would you and Marsha like to ride with me?"

"I can't take her out of school."

"I have a teacher workday on the ninth," Marsha volunteered.

"That's a good day. How about you, Maggie? What's your calendar like?"

"I'll check. I could probably arrange a vacation day if I'm working. And I need to get permission from the caseworker."

"I thought we could visit the zoo. What do you think, Marsha?"

She shrugged.

"You'll like this place," Dillon said.

"Could we invite Mari and the Dennis children?" Maggie requested softly.

Dillon looked disappointed. "I'd hoped to get to know her better."

"Just her?"

Dillon grinned at Maggie. "I've missed you."

"You could have visited."

"I thought Marsha needed you more."

"Okay. We'll do this your way. Just the three of us. What time do you plan to leave?"

"It's a little more than a two-hour drive. I have to go by the courthouse to sign papers, and then we can head for the zoo. How about six thirty or so?"

They made their plans, and early on the morning of their trip, Maggie and Marsha crossed the backyard to Dillon's house for breakfast.

"Thanks for doing this," Maggie said as she took the plate he handed her. "I overslept."

He smiled and winked. "I didn't mind. I got up with the chickens anyway."

"You have chickens?" Marsha asked.

Dillon laughed. "No, honey. That's just something my mama used to say about getting up early. Roosters were their alarm clocks. They'd be up doing chores when that old bird cock-a-doodle-dooed."

"I've never seen a rooster."

"They strut about the yard like they're king of the roost," Maggie said.

"That they do," Dillon agreed, sliding his plate onto the table. "Let's eat so we can get on the road. I'm eager to see the zoo. How about you, Marsha?"

Her head hardly moved in response as she attacked her food. The child ate every meal with such gusto that Maggie wondered how well her mother fed her.

No, she warned herself. The idea that Marsha deserved a better parent teased her, and Maggie already knew she would have problems letting go when the time came. She'd become very attached to the girl in a short time.

Dillon's gaze rested on her, and she picked up her fork and started eating. "This is good," she said, and Marsha nodded.

"Eat up. I made plenty." Dillon rose from the stool and topped off their juice glasses.

As soon as breakfast was over and the dishes were in the dishwasher, Dillon said, "Why don't you ladies finish whatever you need to do and meet me at the car?"

"Come on, Marsha. Let's brush our teeth and comb our hair."

"Don't be long, or I'll leave without you," Dillon joked.

The child looked nervous. Maggie rested her hand on Marsha's shoulder. "He's teasing, honey. He really wants us to go with him. We'll be right back, Dillon."

"I'll wait," he promised solemnly.

Within minutes, they were on the road. Dillon had poured coffee into travel mugs and placed juice boxes in a cooler for Marsha.

Maggie noted how Dillon's gaze frequently went to the rearview mirror and the child reflected there. "Bet you're glad to have a day off from school. I loved teacher workdays. Of course, it's been a long time since I had one. How do you like school?"

When she shrugged, Maggie said, "You need to answer Mr. Rogers. He can't look at you while he's driving."

"Okay," Marsha mumbled.

"A woman of few words," he said softly to Maggie. She nodded.

They arrived in Columbia a little after nine o'clock. Dillon found the courthouse and parked. "Did you want to come in or wait here?"

"We could visit the ladies' room," Maggie said.

"I'm not sure how long this will take." He handed her his car keys.

Dillon concluded his business quickly, and they drove over to Riverbanks Zoo and Garden. He paid their admittance fee and accepted the brochures.

As they strolled through the area, Dillon reached into his pocket. "I have something for you, Marsha."

He handed her a small digital camera. "The printer is at my house. Take all the pictures you want. We'll print them off when we get home. I can take some of you to send to your mom in your next letter."

Why didn't I think of that? Maggie wondered. Maybe because she didn't want to encourage interaction with the mother while she was in jail. That wasn't fair. If it were her parents, she would want to see them. Perhaps she should ask the caseworker about visitation.

"I plan to give her the camera and printer for her birthday," Dillon told Maggie.

"I don't know if her mother can afford it," Maggie said.

"I hadn't considered that."

Maggie watched Marsha as she worked the digital camera the way Dillon had showed her, checking each picture in the viewfinder before taking the photo. "It's a great idea for today. She can take her photos, and you can help her print them. I doubt Marsha has had much quality time with a good father figure, so that will be nice, too."

The child insisted that Dillon and Maggie pose at the monkey cage. Marsha giggled when Dillon waved his arms and scratched his head.

"Hey, I want a copy of that one," Dillon enthused when Marsha ran over to share the image on the camera. "That fellow likes Maggie's golden hair."

Marsha nodded and giggled again.

The next hours were some of the best Maggie could ever recall. When Marsha had filled the camera with photos, Dillon pulled another memory card from his pocket and sent her off to take more pictures.

"The ink to print all those is going to break you."

Dillon shrugged. "It's worth it if it makes her happy. Let's take a breather. All this walking is wearing me out."

"Are you feeling okay?" Maggie asked, afraid the activity had been too much for him. "Everything healed up nicely?"

"My doctor says so. Those staples were the worst."

"But you grimaced and took it like a man?"

"Sure I did. After the initial 'Hey, that hurts,' I became an iron man."

Maggie laughed. "I'm so glad you're feeling better. I worried about you. And thanks for this idea. You've really made Marsha happy."

"Every child should feel that way every day," Dillon said.

"I doubt she's had much opportunity to feel special in her life. Not with a mother who has problems."

"You don't know that to be a fact," he quickly pointed out. "Her mother could be the most loving woman in the world who messed up one time."

"That's all it takes to ruin someone's life."

"Don't hold a lapse in good judgment against the woman," Dillon warned.

Maggie had prayed over her feelings regarding Marsha's mother. For the life of her, she couldn't understand how any mother could allow a man to separate her and her daughter. No mother should do that to her child. As far as Maggie was concerned, a parent should put her child first.

Marsha ran back to where they sat on benches. She paused in front of Dillon, her expression happy when she asked, "Will you come to my party?"

He nodded. "Sure. If you want me to. I'm kind of old, though."

The child leaned against his leg. "You're my friend. Maggie said I could invite my friends."

A knot formed in Maggie's throat as she watched them together.

"I'd be honored. What should I bring you? Tell me your favorite things."

Dillon paid a great deal of attention to the child as she told him about her life. "It's just me and my mom. We take care of each other. I'd like to give her something special, too."

"What did you have in mind?" he asked, and Marsha shrugged. "Why don't we think about it and decide later," he suggested.

As the child's hand slipped into Dillon's, Maggie couldn't help but wonder what made the child bond so quickly with him. What was it about him that charmed the female species?

She'd grown to care for Dillon Rogers in a way she'd never cared for another man. A way that had her thinking about their future. But how could it work? They were worlds apart.

"Maggie?"

"Yes?" she responded, jumping guiltily as she shifted from daydreams to reality.

"Marsha and I were discussing lunch. Would you like a hot dog?"

"Sounds good."

All too soon, their day was over. Hearing Marsha chatter about what she'd seen and the pictures she'd taken made Maggie even happier. Their silent girl had opened up.

When Marsha grew quiet, Maggie glanced back to find she'd fallen asleep. Marsha's head rested against the seat, the long arms of the monkey Dillon had given her wrapped about her neck just as he'd placed the stuffed animal she'd chosen.

"I've never heard her talk so much," she whispered to Dillon. "You made her day."

"How about you? How was your day?"

"I enjoyed myself. I love the zoo. I plan to go back and visit the gardens."

"We could have done that today."

Maggie shook her head. "Marsha wouldn't have enjoyed them as much. I'd come back to the zoo, too."

"And bring the Dennis children?"

"It would make a great educational outing. I could see them there."

"Terrorizing the animals?"

"They're good kids," Maggie objected. "What scares you most? Luke and his questions?"

"The numbers," Dillon said. "I prefer one-on-one like today. And yes, Luke petrifies me. I'm afraid he'll find out I don't know anything."

"Oh, I doubt that. Luke tells everyone you're smart. He always searches you out."

"He likes hearing about my camel rides."

"So do I. You know there are going to be more kids one of these days. Julie and Kimberly are both planning to start families."

Dillon glanced at her. "Does that bother you?"

"Not really. It just changes our relationships. It's hard to get together when children are involved."

"But these children have willing fathers who I'm sure will take over so their wives can have time with their friends."

"I hope so. I enjoy spending time with them."

"You'll still have Natalie. And me. I'm single."

"And not likely to become a mother anytime soon," Maggie countered with a big grin.

Dillon laughed loudly, and Marsha jumped in the backseat. "Sorry, honey. Maggie made me laugh."

She rubbed her eyes. "Are we there yet?"

"Almost. Why don't you get us a juice box out of the cooler?"

Marsha dug juice boxes from the melting ice and busied herself putting in straws and passing them around.

Dillon took a sip. "Ah, that's good. What plans do you ladies have for the weekend?"

"We have chores in the morning, and then I thought we'd go shopping for party items. We need to pick a theme."

"That sounds like fun. Are you interested in burgers and hot dogs for the guests? I could fire up my new grill."

"What do you think, Marsha?"

"Yes. And cake and ice cream and candy."

Maggie glanced at her. "Whoa. That's a serious sugar rush. How about some veggies?" Marsha grimaced. "Maybe lettuce and tomato for the burgers?"

"Okay."

Maggie would let the other parents worry about getting veggies into their kids. "I think we should have a menu. What's your favorite cake?"

"Chocolate."

"Mine, too."

"Is Natalie making the cake?" Dillon asked.

"What do you think?"

"Well, there's always Avery."

Maggie shook her head. "Marsha will have a cake to remember this birthday. Natalie's already planning."

"Then I can only imagine what she will come up with."

"Whatever Marsha wants. Once we pick the theme and decorations, Natalie will design the cake."

"Gives me something to look forward to."

"When's your birthday?" Maggie asked.

"December eighth."

She nodded. "I'll have to share that with Natalie and see what happens. Your favorite cake?"

"Orange."

Long after she'd tucked Marsha in for the night, Maggie found herself still awake. She turned on the lamp and picked up her Bible, reading scriptures and thanking God for the wonderful day He'd given them. Marsha could hardly wait to see the other kids so she could tell them about the zoo. Maybe once Dillon got the photos printed, she could show them.

Memories of the experience with Dillon that day made her smile. He had been so thoughtful and focused on them having fun. She hoped he enjoyed himself, as well. God was so good. She'd been so alone, and now she had a child living in her house and another good friend. She felt very blessed.

ten

The theme was flower power.

And Natalie had not only baked a larger cake for the birthday girl; she'd given the kids their own smaller cupcake versions as well. There were even iced flower cookies. More than one kid would be on a sugar high before the afternoon ended.

After taking Marsha's gift to the church fellowship hall, Dillon went to Maggie's to retrieve the plate of burgers and hot dogs. "Everything looks nice."

"Marsha's so excited. She barely slept last night. She's never had a party. It won't be long before she's gone," Maggie said glumly.

"You heard from her caseworker?"

She nodded, feeling the growing knot in her throat. Dillon folded Maggie into a hug. They stood silently for several seconds before Marsha bounded into the room wearing the tie-dyed T-shirt that she and Maggie had made along with bell-bottomed jeans that sported big flower patches on the legs. A peace symbol dangled on a long string about her neck, and she wore big plastic flower rings on her fingers.

"Hello, birthday girl," Dillon said. The child beamed at him. He lifted the plate from the counter and said, "I'll bring these over to the fellowship hall."

"Thanks, Dillon."

Later, he stood by Maggie's side as they watched a mob of kids run around. "You didn't go crazy by much, did you?"

"It's been fun. The caseworker is taking her to visit her mom tomorrow."

"Are you okay with that?"

"I have to be. When Marsha looks back at her time with

me, I think she'll remember this party. And the zoo trip."

"I found a special gift for her to share with her mom."

Excited, Maggie turned to him and asked, "Really? What?"

"Two necklaces with one heart charm. Each of them gets half."

"That's perfect!" Maggie exclaimed. She threw her arms about his neck and kissed his cheek.

"Whoa," Dillon said, his arm slipping about Maggie's waist before allowing his lips to touch hers gently. Remembering where they were, they parted and took a step back.

Maggie turned pink. "Sorry, I didn't mean to attack you."

"Are you truly sorry?" he asked softly.

She wiped the lipstick smudge from his cheek. "No."

"I love you, Maggie."

Her eyes widened. She loved him, too. It had come slowly, creeping up on them, and she knew as surely as she drew her next breath that he held her heart. "Let's talk about this later. After the party."

"Definitely," Dillon promised with a tender smile.

He loved her. Maggie felt as if she were walking on air. What exactly did that mean? They were both a bit old to go steady, weren't they? Oh well, maybe not.

It thrilled her that he'd taken the little girl's wish for something special to share with her mother and made it happen. Maggie considered her own wishes. She'd wished for a home ever since her dad had died. Could Dillon give her that?

"Those kids are going to mutiny if we don't get the games under way," Dillon told her.

She and Marsha had found the perfect party games and then had fun at the dollar store finding prizes for the winners. Marsha would be able to plan her own parties in the future if her mom fell short. Particularly her sweet sixteen. Maggie paused as she considered that leap into adulthood. Marsha was only eleven. Thirteen would be the next milestone.

Why couldn't she have met Dillon Rogers years ago when

she could have had children of her own to guide through these milestones?

Because it wasn't meant to be. She refused to live her life crying over spilt milk. Look for the positives. Tonight when she wrote in her gratitude journal, she'd be thankful that she'd given one little girl a happy day, but she'd be joyous over the good friends in her life and now the love of one special man. What could be better than that?

"Whew," Dillon exclaimed later as he stuffed the last trash bag in the Dumpster. "What a day. Where's Marsha?"

"She wanted to watch her new DVD with the Dennis kids. I told Mari I'd pick her up when I finished here."

"So have you thought any more about what I told you earlier?"

She looked at him. "A time or two."

"And what are you going to do about it?" he challenged.

"What do you suggest?"

"You could return the sentiment."

"And if I did?"

"Who knows what would happen."

Reality washed over her. "I do care for you, Dillon. A great deal."

He lifted one brow and asked, "But you aren't using the *L* word just yet."

" 'I love you' has never been easy for me to say," Maggie admitted.

"What do you want, Maggie?"

"To feel I've come home."

"Tell me what that means."

"A place where I belong, where I feel loved and protected. The place we come to and know we're important to everyone there."

"How do you know when you're there?"

"You just do."

"That's an ambiguous response."

Sadness encompassed Maggie as her description fell short

of making him understand. "If I knew how to explain it better, I would."

"Let me give it a shot. I think you mean like when I was in first grade and a bully picked on me and I knew my mom would take my side."

"Exactly. A dragon slayer."

"I'll slay your dragons, Maggie. Just share them with me."

She rested her hand against his cheek. "You've done a wonderful job, Dillon. That damage to the house was a dragon. You took care of that. This party was a dragon. You've helped so much today."

"And do you feel like coming home?"

"I'm closer than I've ever been. I'd better get Marsha home. I'm sure she's exhausted."

"Can I walk with you?"

Maggie slipped her arm through his. "I wouldn't expect anything less from my dragon slayer."

He laughed and worked his fingers through hers.

"Natalie did a fantastic job with that cake. I'm thinking about placing a weekly order so I can have it for dessert every day."

She stared at him and then burst out laughing. "I'm sure Marsha will share her cake if you come to lunch tomorrow."

"I thought the caseworker was taking her to see her mom."

Maggie sighed. "I forgot. Oh well, come over anyway, and we'll drown our sorrows in leftover birthday cake."

eleven

"Marsha's gone."

Maggie's heartbroken expression and the tears on her lashes tore at Dillon. "I didn't want you hurt. I liked Marsha."

"I'm sorry." She sniffed and grabbed another tissue. She'd used a box since saying good-bye to the child that morning. "You should go home. I'm not fit company."

"Let's do something to take your mind off what's happened. How about getting together with friends and going out to dinner?"

"I wouldn't be good company."

"Didn't you divert Marsha's attention to keep her from missing her mother?"

"That was different. She's a child."

"And you have to be miserable because you're an adult?"

"Don't be silly."

"I'm only trying to help, Maggie. If you continue to act as a foster parent, you'll have to love them enough to let them go. Pray for her. Pray that her mom will turn their lives around in a good way. You took her to church. Now Marsha knows about God's love. She's never been exposed to that before."

"I want to be happy for Marsha," she whispered. "I really do."

Dillon hugged her. "So about those friends and dinner."

Maggie shook her head.

"Do you want me to go?" Dillon asked gently.

Maggie grasped his hand and shook her head.

"Come on. We need to get out of here. How about a show at one of the musical theaters? We could play putt-putt or go fishing. Tell me something you've always wanted to do."

"Ripley's." Other than she'd always thought she'd go one day, Maggie had no idea why it had popped into her head now.

"You're on. I'll get the car."

"Give me a few minutes to get myself together."

An hour later, Maggie pointed at the pamphlet and laughed. "Look, Dillon, they call it an Odditorium."

He grabbed her hand, pulling her through the turnstile and to the first display. They had the place to themselves as they moved up stairs that glowed in the dark and through a labyrinth of semidark passages, reading the placards describing each exhibit Robert L. Ripley had gathered in his world travels.

"Check him out," Dillon said, indicating the tallest man either of them had ever seen.

They continued, studying the facts, viewing the illusions, examining Cleopatra's barge made entirely out of sugar, as well as a matchstick roller coaster, oddities of nature, and artwork made of everything from jellybeans to butterfly wings.

"Look at this," Maggie said, indicating a picture of Jesus with the book of John written in the background.

Dillon leaned closer and said, "You can actually read the words."

Maggie shuddered at the old torture devices on display.

When they approached a bridge that warned them to enter if they dared, Maggie looked askance at the walls that seemed to turn about them.

"Come on," Dillon said. They stepped onto the bridge, and she found that it moved from side to side.

They entered a room and sat on the benches and watched videos of outstanding feats.

"Marsha would like this place." She grew silent as the sadness returned. "Do you think she's okay?"

"Yeah, I do. Marsha's a tough kid."

"She's just a little girl."

"Who had to grow up faster than most. Like you, Maggie."

"I wish it could be different for her."

"It is. She has a mother to love and care for her."

Her anger peaked, shattering the last shreds of her control.

"Much better than a foster parent."

"I didn't say that," Dillon said quickly. "God blessed Marsha with you at the time when she needed you most. She knew you cared and took that knowledge and those memories home with her. You planted the seed of Jesus in her heart, and we both know what God can do."

Shamed by her angry outburst, Maggie said, "I hope so. I want her to be happy."

He took her hand in his and asked, "Are you sure foster parenting is right for you? I don't like the thought of seeing you heartbroken every time you lose a child."

They sat in silence for a couple of minutes, idly watching the television screen. "I suppose in time I'll learn to protect my heart, to accept that I'm making a difference by just being there and loving my fellow man as God directs."

"How about you love as freely as you like and let me help protect your heart?"

Confused, she looked at him. "How. . ." she began, trailing off when Dillon slipped off the bench onto one knee.

"I love you, Maggie. I want to marry you." He held her hand in his, and the firm grip made her feel protected. "I thank God for blessing me with you in my life."

"You really mean that?" Maggie asked. "You're thankful for me?"

"Very much so."

"Why do you want to marry me?"

"I want to be your husband," he said simply. "To love you. To share your generous heart. To be the one you come home to."

"I love you, Dillon. I didn't want to, but I couldn't help myself. It came as naturally as breathing. Well, actually you sneaked up on me and knocked me breathless with your love."

"I hope to keep you breathless," Dillon said with a broad smile. He reached into his pocket and removed a jeweler's box. Opening the lid, he held it out to her. The large diamond gleamed in the overhead light.

Maggie hesitated. "Dillon, that's. . ."

He nodded. "Mom's ring. I considered buying a new one but decided this one would mean more. You did tell me to save her jewelry for my wife," he reminded. "I had it cleaned. We can update the setting, or I'll buy you a new ring if that's what you want."

"No, you can't change the ring. It's perfect." Mrs. Allene had worn it with pride for a great number of years. Maggie wanted to do the same.

"Maggie?" he prompted, pushing the box in her direction.

She hesitated. "I'm scared, Dillon. I don't know how to be a good wife."

"I don't know how to be a good husband, either. We can learn together."

Maggie felt so helpless.

"Did you doubt you could be a good foster parent?"

"I had my moments," she admitted.

"But you were willing to try."

"And if I'd failed, they would not have allowed me to have other children. They have a word for failed marriages, too, Dillon."

"I wouldn't have proposed if I wasn't certain about us."

"I don't have doubts about you, Dillon. It's me."

"You don't want to marry me?" he asked, trouble lines appearing in his forehead.

"I do."

"Then say yes," he prompted.

"You realize I'm a fifty-year-old old maid?"

"So I'm the fifty-five-plus male equivalent. I never thought I'd meet the right woman, and now that I have, I don't want to let you go. Remember the vows, Maggie. For better or worse, richer or poorer, in sickness and in health. I'm committed to you. Forever."

She touched his cheek, feeling the bristle of his five o'clock shadow beneath her hand. Tears welled in her eyes as she absorbed the promise he'd just made to her. "Yes, Dillon. I'd love to be your wife."

He rose to his feet and pulled her into his arms. "Thank God. My knee was about to give out."

Maggie flashed him a playful frown. "Now that's not very romantic."

"I'll make it up to you. I didn't intend to propose like this. I wanted it to be someplace special. Done up right."

"This feels pretty right to me," Maggie said.

"You're a cheap date," Dillon said as he reached for her hand and slid the ring in place. It fit perfectly.

"You think so? This looks expensive."

He leaned forward and kissed her. "Romantic?"

"I thought Kim's was big," Maggie said.

"And that's good?"

She tapped him on the chest. "No, silly. It's not the size of the diamond. It's the love that puts it there."

"Well, if we're measuring in love, I couldn't afford the carats to match my feelings for you. Dad gave that to Mom on their twenty-fifth anniversary. He never gave her an engagement ring and looked a long time for the perfect ring."

"That makes it even more special." Maggie twisted her hand back and forth, appreciating the shine of the diamond as it reflected in the light. "Oh, Dillon, I'm like Doubting Thomas when it comes to love. I don't want to be insecure in my love for you, but I am."

"Then let me prove my intentions are honorable. I won't let you down, Maggie."

"I know you won't. I don't doubt that for a moment. I'm afraid I'll let you down. Can we tell Mari and Joe?"

Dillon smiled and said, "I thought you didn't feel like seeing anyone."

Maggie remembered Marsha and felt guilty.

"I think we should," Dillon said quickly. "When do you want to get married?"

"Probably early next year."

"So long?" Dillon countered with a frown.

"Well, I want to be married at Cornerstone, and Joe requires marital counseling. That takes some time."

"How about Valentine's Day?" Dillon suggested.

Maggie nodded. "We can say our vows after church the Sunday before Valentine's Day."

"You sure you don't want all the trimmings?"

Maggie paused for a moment as thoughts of her childhood dream wedding filled her head. "I'm too old for all that."

"No, honey, you're never too old for anything you want to do," Dillon countered.

"I would look silly," she objected. "We'll be just as married with a simple wedding as an expensive one."

"Whatever you want," Dillon said amicably.

What do I want? Maggie wondered. Definitely to marry Dillon. She loved him a great deal.

"We can live in Mom's house and rent yours."

That caught her attention.

"It's not like that," he protested immediately upon seeing her expression. "The house is yours. I don't have anything to do with the property."

"But what about two becoming one?" Maggie asked. How could she marry him if she doubted his actions? "I don't have lots of worldly possessions, but what I do have will belong to us both. Including the house."

He lifted her hand to his lips. "I don't want anything to stand in the way of our happiness. My possessions will belong to you, too. I plan to change my will."

"Let's do it together," Maggie suggested.

Dillon took her hand, and they continued their tour. As they exited onto the stairs leading to the game room, he asked, "Feel better?"

Maggie smiled at him and nodded. "Much."

twelve

Maggie Gregory was getting married.

That was the buzz around the community, her church, and her job. She'd flashed her beautiful diamond more than she could imagine and never tired of the comments.

It seemed like a dream. Maggie Gregory had caught a man. Incredible. A wealthy, handsome one at that. Who would have thought it could happen? Certainly not her.

Mari and Joe had been delighted for them both. When Joe insisted on putting them on the calendar for counseling after the first of the year, neither she nor Dillon protested. They might be older and wiser in some respects, but neither of them knew what to expect when it came to marriage. Maggie planned on forever and knew this was a step in the right direction.

She was talking with Mari when Julie, Natalie, Kimberly, and Peg found them after service on Sunday morning.

"I'm so happy for you," Julie cried, hugging Maggie. "When did he propose? Details. We need details."

"The day Marsha went home to her mother. I was so blue, and he took me to Ripley's and got down on one knee and proposed right there."

"Believe it or not?" Kimberly teased.

"Oh, believe me, I'm still pinching myself. It doesn't seem real."

"Well, that ring is. It's beautiful," Julie said.

"It was Mrs. Allene's," Maggie said, twisting her hand side to side.

"Dillon obviously loves you. It doesn't get better than that. So what do you plan for the wedding?" Julie asked.

"Very simple. We're standing up after Sunday morning

services to say our vows."

"What?" they all chorused.

"It's what we want."

"Is it?" Julie demanded. "There are no memories in that kind of ceremony. You might as well go to the wedding chapel in Dillon, South Carolina."

"It's best for us both. And I will have memories. We'll be married in our church home by our pastor," Maggie told her.

"And you'll make more memories," Mari consoled upon realizing that Julie's argument troubled their friend.

"That's right. Dillon's planning our honeymoon, and there's no telling where we'll end up."

"I wouldn't take anything for my wedding memories," Kim said.

"Me, either," Julie agreed. "We may have put the wedding together in a week, but it was beautiful."

"Maybe I'm just too practical to be romantic," Maggie said. "Big weddings are for young girls. Not old women like me."

Dillon waved at her from across the room. "I have to go. Dillon's taking me to lunch with his family. See you tonight."

&

After Maggie left with her new fiancé, Julie cried, "We can't let her do this."

"It's not our decision," Mari reminded.

"We'll see," Julie countered.

The women looked at each other and groaned. What was Julie thinking? They were all more than a little familiar with her escapades.

"Ready, honey?" Noah asked.

"Oh, I'm more than ready," she said, grinning at the others before she took his arm and walked out of the church.

"I don't like this," Mari said, obviously worried that her sister-in-law would do something foolish. "You know how Julie is."

Kim shrugged. "She's right. Maggie deserves more than this little nothing wedding she's planning."

"We can pray over it," Mari said. "But we need to respect Maggie and Dillon's decision."

"We need to talk some sense into her," Natalie said. "Why would they choose to get married at the time when everyone is eager to get home to their lunch? Even something simple in the afternoon for a group of their close friends would be better."

"It's Maggie and Dillon's wedding," Mari reminded yet again.

"But do you honestly think it's the best choice for a wedding ceremony?" Kim asked her.

"I'd prefer that they do something more special," Mari admitted.

"Then we need to convince Maggie to change her mind," Kim said. "I'm going to talk to Julie this week and see what she's thinking."

thirteen

"When do you have days off again?" Dillon asked.

"The first of the week. I work next weekend. Why do you ask?"

"I wanted to visit Charleston. How about Monday? We could leave early and make a day of it."

"What's in Charleston?" Maggie asked curiously.

"Lots of history," he enthused. "Fort Sumter. Horse-and-buggy tours. Boat and bus tours, too. What do you think?"

There were a million things she needed to do, but Maggie decided she'd rather spend the day with Dillon. "Sounds wonderful as long as we don't spend all day at that fort place."

"We can stop at Mount Pleasant and visit Boone Hall Plantation if you like."

"I've never been to Charleston. My foster parents took me all around DC when I lived with them, but I've never had much opportunity to do the tourist thing here."

"You don't take vacations?"

"Now and then. Usually I stayed home and worked on whatever project I had going at the time. You'll find I'm more of a homebody than world traveler."

"There's never been anywhere you wanted to go?"

"Not that I could afford. I did the cruise thing once. And I've been to Disney with a couple of church groups."

"So if you could go anywhere you wanted, where would you go?"

Maggie considered the question. "I don't know. Australia maybe."

"What about Europe? China?"

"You've seen those places?"

Dillon nodded. Another difference between them, Maggie

considered glumly. How could he be content with someone like her?

"I've done more than my share of exploring," Dillon said. "I'd like to show you my favorite places, but I'm ready to keep my feet planted on solid ground if that's what you want. We'll take it slow. You'll have fun. I promise."

And Dillon kept that promise. On Monday they headed for Charleston. Their first stop was Boone Hall Plantation in Mount Pleasant. As they drove along the world's longest oak-lined avenue to the house, Maggie said, "I feel like I'm heading for Tara. Or was it Twelve Oaks? Come to think of it, I don't think Tara had trees like these."

"I wouldn't know."

Maggie looked at him. "You never saw *Gone with the Wind*?"

"Never."

"Well, that's a part of your education I can remedy. I have the movie on tape. It's four hours long."

Dillon looked surprised. "You're kidding."

"It has an intermission."

For the next hour, they toured America's most photographed plantation, learning the history of the Low Country estate and still-working plantation.

"So what do you think? Would you like a house like this?" Dillon whispered as they followed the guide.

Maggie shook her head. "Give me cozy and quaint anytime."

"Me, too."

They drove the six miles into Charleston.

Dillon marveled over the incredible bridge. "I read that it's the longest cable-stayed bridge in the nation."

Their next stop was at the visitor's center. After studying what was available, Maggie said, "We can visit the fort first. I know you're eager to do that."

"This says the tour is two and a half hours long. Let's pick a Charleston tour so we can see the city."

His willingness to please her did all sorts of things to Maggie's heart.

Later, after they visited Fort Sumter, Maggie commented on his obvious interest in history. "Tell me what else you like," she said. Puzzlement touched his face. "I know you like to travel."

He took her hand in his. "I like spending time with you."

"Good thing," Maggie teased. "I'll soon be around twenty-four hours a day. You'll get a break on the days I work."

He brought her hand up to his lips. "I'll miss you on those days."

She smiled at his romantic gesture. "I'll miss you, too. So what else do you like?"

Dillon held on to her hand as they walked around. "Staying busy, mostly. I thought that once I get the house finished, I might offer to head up a small home repair group at the church. For seniors and single moms. What do you think?"

"It's a good mission. And will probably keep you busier than you realize."

"I thought maybe some of the other guys might be interested. Wyatt's helping Kim with her Christmas program plans, but he's not interested in the choir. He'd like to help others in some way, as well."

It thrilled Maggie that her future husband was a godly man who cared about others.

After lunch they caught the next bus tour. Maggie noted that all their tour guides today were well versed in their ability to share Charleston's history. Their driver showed them various aspects of South Carolina's second most populous city. They toured historic houses and a theater before they were delivered back to the visitor's center. It was getting late by the time they left Charleston.

"What are you looking for?" Dillon asked as she rummaged through her purse.

"My cell phone. I must have left it charging at home. I wanted to check my voice mail."

He unclipped his from his belt and handed it to her.

There was one message, and Maggie immediately recognized

Mrs. Prince's voice. "They want to place two small children with me," she said after listening to the caseworker's message.

"When do you have time to care for two children, work, and plan a wedding?"

"What plans are there beyond buying a dress and you getting a new suit?"

"What about our counseling sessions?"

"What's going on, Dillon? You obviously don't want me to take these children."

"You have a lot going on right now," he said smoothly, with no expression on his face.

"So are you being protective or selfish?"

He looked sheepish. "A little of both. I want to spend time with you. It's difficult when you're caring for children."

"But I enjoyed my time with Marsha. And Chloe."

Dillon glanced at her and said, "And got your heart broken."

"All of them don't leave so soon," Maggie objected. "What's the real problem? Are you saying you don't want me to be a foster parent?"

He glanced at her and asked, "What if I said yes? Would you choose being a foster parent over being my wife?"

Maggie frowned and shook her head. "No. I like providing a secure loving home to the children who need them, but to continue after we're married, you'll have to be part of the experience. I realize that's probably something you haven't had time to consider."

"I don't know what to say, Maggie. I'm an old guy who has never been exposed to children. I'm not a father or an uncle. Very few of my friends had children, so when you talk about parenting, it's really something I don't know if I want or not."

He spoke freely about his feelings, and Maggie did the same. "My experience is limited to my friends' children and the church nursery, but it proved worthwhile."

"And no doubt I'd find it just as worthwhile, but right now there are things I want more."

"Like what?"

"Time with you. Maybe I am selfish, but I want more than a few days between placements. Most newlyweds take time before they start families. I know we're not so young anymore, but I'd still like my couple time."

"I understand, Dillon. Truly I do. It's just that I feel I'd be letting the program down."

He sighed. "Maybe it's because I haven't had time to adapt to the idea. I'm sure you were 100 percent behind the plan from day one, but I'm trying to decide how I feel."

"Is it because they're foster kids?"

"Good grief, Maggie, don't you think I have enough sense to know how blessed I was to have good parents?" he demanded. "And to realize that not everyone is that fortunate?"

"That's why I want to do this," she explained. "To help those kids."

Dillon pulled into the opposite lane to pass a slow-moving vehicle. "Can we at least adapt to married life before you add another person to the mix?"

His reluctance troubled her. "It took months to get approved for foster care. I just started."

A few moments of silence elapsed before Dillon spoke. "It sounds sappy, but I just found you. I don't particularly care to share you all the time."

And romantic, Maggie thought as she suggested, "I don't want you feeling overwhelmed, either. How about for now, I take only short-term placements—for children who need a place until the wedding—and then we can look at it again later next year?"

He glanced at her and smiled. "After the long honeymoon I plan to take you on. Anywhere you want to go."

"The place doesn't matter, Dillon. Just so long as we're together."

He reached for her hand. "Hearing you say that makes me even more determined to do something truly outrageous. Maybe even a trip around the world."

"I do have a job, you know."

"Yes," he acknowledged glumly. "That's something I'd love to change."

"What if I found a job at a doctor's office?" Maggie asked.

"Part-time?"

"Maybe if I rented the house and got enough income to offset my expenses. I wouldn't be able to contribute much to our budget, though."

"I can support you."

"Do you have any idea what you're suggesting?"

"It would give us more time together."

"Yes. Maybe too much time. We need to think about this. Pray over it."

"So we put that on the list with foster care for later discussion?"

"I think so. Not that I'm totally opposed to the idea of not working," she admitted with a little laugh.

Soon they turned onto their street. Dillon parked in his driveway and escorted her home. Her words swirled in his head as he unlocked his back door. When he'd realized he was in love with Maggie Gregory, he decided to make her part of his life. He hadn't calculated children into the mix.

How did he really feel about being a foster parent? Dillon knew Maggie would expect an answer to her question sooner than later. And he truly didn't have one.

In the kitchen, he took a glass from the cabinet and filled it with ice and water from the new stainless steel refrigerator he'd recently bought. His house was certainly up to code with all the renovations he'd done.

Admittedly, getting to know Marsha had been nice. She was a sweet child, but it was more than the kids. He wanted time with Maggie, not the world. Already she had a multitude of friends that filled much of her off time.

That was something else in the way—her job. He didn't care for sitting around, waiting for her to get off work and then hoping she wasn't too tired to spend time with him. If she didn't have to work, they could travel and see the places she'd never seen. Being foster parents wouldn't allow that. They'd be stuck in Myrtle Beach.

Would Maggie understand his selfish desire to have her to himself? Maybe after a year or so, they could foster kids again, but first he wanted time alone with the woman he loved. That wasn't too much to ask, was it?

❧

Maggie glanced at the clock and headed for the shower. She'd enjoyed their trip. Dillon was a lot of fun. Things had gone well until she'd called home to check her messages.

She'd assumed Dillon would be willing to continue foster parenting after they married. Of course, she hadn't considered the intrusion on his privacy with the check-in visits by the caseworkers and having children around all the time. He had gotten along well with Marsha, but then he hadn't been around her that much. Was it reasonable to ask this of him? She could tell Dillon that if he loved her, he would agree, but that wasn't fair to him.

And just as she'd adapted to Marsha, Maggie knew it would take time for them to adapt to living together. She hated to let the foster care program down, but she needed to be fair to Dillon. He said he'd think about foster parenting, but she wouldn't pressure him.

If Dillon wanted to do this, they would proceed. Otherwise, she'd do what she could to help before the wedding. Content with her decision, Maggie turned on the hair dryer.

❧

A few days later, Mari asked, "You and Dillon are coming for Thanksgiving dinner, aren't you?"

Mari had issued an invitation days before, but Maggie hesitated. "You have family coming."

"It's just us. Julie and Noah are visiting his parents that weekend. Julie wants to spend Christmas with her Cornerstone family. Last year's Christmas celebration at the church was such a success that we're planning to do the same thing again."

The year before when Luke had destroyed Mari's list, Julie planned Christmas dinner for everyone at Cornerstone who didn't have special plans.

"Has she already started on Joe about the kid's gifts?" Maggie asked.

"You know she has," Mari said, her voice filled with loving exasperation. "She wants to buy them one of those huge blow-up slides and a ball pit for the backyard. So when Joe says we don't have storage, she offers to buy a building. Honestly, I don't know how Joe refuses. She offers the most convincing arguments."

"You think they'll spoil their own kids?"

"You know they will. Noah tries to curb her generosity, but there are times even he can't refuse her."

Julie's talent for software design and her investment in her employer's company had provided her with more than enough money to share. "Particularly when she's doing so much good for others?"

Mari nodded. "I know the kids would love the slide, but it's not practical."

"But you know she'll come up with something equally as good, don't you?"

Mari grinned and nodded. "Did I tell you Joe's taking the singing Santa over to their place while they're away?"

The Santa had been yet another of Julie's inspirations for the kids. The motion detector activated the thing every time someone came near.

Maggie laughed. "She'll be surprised it's still around. She was sure you'd sell it at a yard sale."

"I'm afraid it's going to set them both off with the practical jokes. So will you come?" Mari asked.

"You have your hands full with Joe and the kids."

"You could always relieve some of the burden. Another set of hands would be appreciated."

"Okay. I'll ask Dillon. But only if you let me contribute to the meal."

"We'll plan a menu with all our traditions."

"Sounds good, but I don't have any traditions. Perhaps you can share a few of yours."

"I imagine you and Dillon will come up with a few of your own. But you can start with Mrs. Allene's mac and cheese casserole. It would be a perfect addition to Thanksgiving dinner."

"Ah, so that's the real reason you want me to come," she teased.

"The real reason is because you're my friend and the kids will love you forever."

"You got it. What else should I bring?"

❧

Thanksgiving with the Dennis family had proved enjoyable. Maggie wasn't sure, but she felt Dillon had become more comfortable around the kids. They certainly seemed to enjoy his company.

When she'd talked with her caseworker the day after their trip, Maggie learned they placed the children with another family when she wasn't available. She explained her situation, and Mrs. Prince said she'd keep Maggie in mind, but there hadn't been another placement.

She zipped her jacket and pulled on a pair of gloves. "I can't believe Christmas is in two weeks." Colder than usual weather had certainly put a zip in the day they had chosen to visit Simpson's Tree Farm. "Are you sure you don't want a tree?"

"Just a wreath for the door. I might put out one of those ceramic trees Mom had. That's enough."

"Not for me," Maggie declared. "I love to decorate for the holidays. I got a later start than usual this year."

"And you plan on catching up this weekend?"

She pulled a list from her pocket and read, "Tree, garlands, wreath. That's a beginning. The other stuff comes out when I unpack my coat closet, which never sees a coat."

"Let's go. I'll drive."

Upon their arrival at the farm, Dillon reached for her hand and said, "Let's go find your tree."

A couple of hours later they found the perfect one. "This is it," Maggie pronounced.

"You're sure?"

Maggie had already picked and discarded numerous trees. "Positive. I'll stand right here while you get Mr. Simpson. I don't want to risk not being able to find it again."

Minutes later, Dillon grinned at her childlike exuberance when she grabbed the tip of the netted tree and walked toward the car. She sang Christmas carols and stepped aside while the men fitted the tree into the trunk. They walked over to a display of evergreen wreaths, and she chose the largest one on the rack along with six garlands.

Dillon chose a smaller wreath and reached for his wallet. "What's the total?"

"I'll pay for mine," Maggie said.

"I plan to enjoy your tree, so it's only fair that I pay," Dillon offered.

She shrugged, and the two men came to an agreement.

"Julie came by yesterday with Mari and the boys," Mr. Simpson told them.

"Does this year's tree rival last year's?" Maggie asked with a big grin.

Mr. Simpson laughed. "The boys tried, but she didn't fall for it this time."

On the ride home, Maggie told Dillon the story of the monstrous tree the Dennis boys had talked their aunt Julie into buying the previous year.

"It was the biggest, ugliest tree on the farm. Then Luke let the cat out of the bathroom and ended up turning the monstrous tree over on Julie. Noah can hardly tell the story without laughing. He said the look on Julie's face was priceless. They'll never celebrate another Christmas without that story being told."

At Maggie's, they worked at getting the tree into a stand.

Following Maggie's instructions, Dillon rearranged the furniture and centered the tree in front of her new windows.

"Perfect."

"Where are the lights?" When Maggie pointed to a plastic bin that contained several strands, he asked, "All of those?"

"A tree needs lights," she defended. "I wrap every branch."

Dillon pulled the first reel of lights from the box. "You really don't mess around, do you?"

"I pack them away in good working order." She took the reel and laid it to the side. "Those are twinklers. They go on last."

"Okay, you wrap. I'll keep them untangled and follow."

Much later, when Maggie declared the completed tree the most beautiful ever, Dillon agreed with her. "You almost make me want one of my own."

"You should. Your mother has some beautiful ornaments. I used to help with her tree, too."

"What do you think about adding some of them to this tree?"

"And making it our first tree?"

"Sounds good to me," Dillon agreed.

"Me, too," Maggie said with a happy sigh. "I love Christmas. I have all sorts of plans for the holidays. You are coming to the Christmas Day dinner at church, aren't you?"

He nodded. "Leslie invited us, but I told her we had plans."

Dillon had taken her to Leslie's home for lunch right after they announced their engagement. She'd enjoyed spending time with his cousin and her family. "Are you sure you wouldn't rather be with your relatives?"

"I'd rather be with you."

Lost in his beautiful blue eyes, Maggie knew he meant every word. "We could go to Leslie's."

"I told her we'd stop by on Christmas Eve. Is that okay?"

Maggie slipped her arms about his waist and hugged him. "It's fine."

"How about a break to admire our handiwork over hot chocolate?"

"Sounds good. You make the chocolate. I'll unpack my figurines," Maggie said.

They sat on the sofa, drinking big mugs of chocolate and discussing the remaining decorations.

"The outside stuff is in the building," Maggie said. "I'll work on that tomorrow."

Early the next morning, Dillon found Maggie hard at work. Several boxes sat in the yard as she systematically organized her outside decorations. Three wire trees stood nearby. "I've already put the net lights on the shrubs."

"Am I going to be able to sleep at night?" Dillon teased after he kissed her.

"Probably not. I will be putting the mega-lights on your side of the house."

"Then don't be surprised if they mysteriously get unplugged."

Maggie grinned at him. As they worked their way into the front yard, Maggie paused to examine the sago palm she'd added last year. "It's not going to survive."

"We'll have to get a replacement. I fixed the fountain."

Maggie whirled around. "It's working?"

Dillon nodded. "You'll have to decide whether it meets your standards."

"I loved that fountain."

"We'll walk over after we finish and see what you think."

ò.

Life was good, Maggie thought as she wrapped her last gift. She'd found some things for Dillon today that she felt certain he would like. She studied the ribbon spools on the table and chose one to match the paper. After tying a big bow and adding Dillon's name to the tag, she placed it beneath the tree.

Because they were going to the church on Christmas Day, Dillon and Maggie had decided to open their gifts to each other on Christmas Eve after they returned from dinner with his family. Dillon had warmed up to the idea of celebrating Christmas. They'd attended the programs at church and the annual parade, and he'd taken her to a holiday show at the theater. They had even visited a couple of neighborhoods to check out their light displays. When Wyatt and Kim mentioned the Nights of a Thousand Candles at Brookgreen Gardens, he'd asked if she wanted to go. He'd even suggested the Festival of Trees at Ripley's Aquarium. Maggie told them there wasn't enough time for everything. He admitted his previous lack of cheer had stemmed from many years of very little celebration in Saudi.

Maggie considered her relationship with Dillon. Feeling loved was so wonderful. She never wanted it to end. But fear was her constant companion. No matter how much she prayed about the situation, she hadn't found total peace. She wanted to be Dillon's wife but feared her insecurities would stand in the way of their happiness.

fourteen

"Hey, Dillon, this is Julie. Can you come over to Mari's today for lunch?"

"Maggie's at work."

Julie laughed. "We know. We're inviting you."

He couldn't help but feel suspicious. "What's up?"

"We'll tell you when you get here. Come around noon. See you then."

Dillon wondered what her friends had in mind as he hung up the phone. It didn't make sense they'd invite him without Maggie. Oh well, he had to eat. And he'd been meaning to discuss his mission idea with Joe. Maybe he'd be around.

Over soup and sandwiches, the women outlined their plan.

The more they talked, the more concerned he became. "I don't know, Julie. I don't feel right about deceiving her."

"It's not deceit," she insisted. "It's surprise. You don't honestly think Maggie wants her wedding to be some little stand-up affair after church, do you?"

"She said she did."

"Only because she believes she doesn't deserve better."

Her statement confused Dillon. "Why would she think that?"

"She thinks people would consider a big wedding for an old maid foolish. We don't agree. Maggie didn't think she'd ever find her Mr. Right. We prayed for her, and God gave her you."

"I want her to be happy. I'll do whatever it takes."

"Then help us make this happen for her," Julie encouraged. "I promise to take the heat if she gets upset. But I don't think she will. She'll be delighted with the end result."

"She's never going to agree. She said simple."

"That's the beauty of our plan. You and Maggie make the

simple plans. We rev them up. And you're not deceiving her. You're helping us surprise her."

"So far the wedding is just us in dress clothes after church. We haven't taken it any further."

"Trust us, Dillon," Mari said. "I felt the same as you at first. But after serious consideration, much prayer, and some conversations with Maggie, I changed my mind. We're her friends. We'd never do anything to hurt her."

"But what if she truly doesn't want a big wedding?"

"She didn't think she wanted a husband, either," Kim pointed out.

"Exactly," Julie agreed. "She didn't believe her prince would ever come."

Dillon looked skeptical. "You wouldn't ask me to dress in tights and ride a white horse, would you?"

They all giggled like little girls at the thought. "Ah, come on, Dillon," Julie teased. "Couldn't you just see Maggie's face?"

He thought about his practical Maggie and all the things she'd missed in life. Her friends were right. She deserved a memorable wedding. "Okay, I'm in. But no tights."

"And we've got it under control," Julie said. "Mari and I are going dress shopping with her next week. What woman can resist trying on wedding gowns? Once she picks her favorite of the real dresses, I'll make sure it's in the dressing room on her wedding day."

"Julie, that's ingenious," Kim declared. "Can I come, too?"

"Me, too," Natalie chimed in.

Mari and Julie glanced at each other and smiled. "The more the merrier. We need one promise from you, Dillon. Every time she acts suspicious, you kiss her and say, 'I can't wait to have you as my wife.'"

"I can handle that."

"Whatever you do, don't give us away," Julie instructed. "Miss Maggie Gregory is about to get the surprise of her life, and she's going to love you for it."

"It may be the stupidest thing I've ever done," Dillon told them.

"Actually, I'd rate it up there with the best," Julie said. "Just wait until you see her on your wedding day. You'll put every doubt behind you."

"We're planning a shower," Mari said.

"We already have more than we need in the two houses, not including what I have in Saudi," Dillon offered.

"A new bride needs pretties," Kim pointed out.

His face turned red.

"We're calling the wedding Project Love Day," Mari said. "We're decorating the church and planning a formal sit-down dinner for the reception. Several women have signed up to provide food. Of course, Maggie will know nothing until it's time to write the thank-you notes."

"And I'm doing your cake as a gift," Natalie said.

"You were doing this with or without my help, weren't you?" Dillon asked, his gaze shifting from woman to woman.

Julie nodded. "If we had to. Maggie's very important to us."

"And to me. I love her a great deal."

He noted the way the women smiled at each other.

"Where are you taking her on your honeymoon?" Natalie asked.

Dillon shrugged. "I don't know. I've suggested a few places, but she doesn't seem interested."

"Why not Saudi? She'd love to see where you lived, meet your friends, help sort through your stuff."

"That's not a honeymoon," he objected.

"You'll find Maggie's idea of a honeymoon is being with you wherever you are," Mari said.

"There's always the Alaskan cruise she's talked about," Kim said.

"Or Australia. Remember she has the pen pal friend over there," Mari pointed out.

"Why can't Maggie tell me this?"

"Maggie isn't a *me* kind of person, but every once in a

while she shares a tidbit about herself. You have to pay close attention or you'll miss it."

Dillon believed that. She'd surprised him more than once. Hopefully he could keep his mouth shut and not spoil this for Maggie or her friends.

❧

"So what's the plan for your day off?" Dillon asked Sunday night before leaving for the evening.

"The girls are taking me dress shopping."

"Want to come over for breakfast? I could make one of those omelets you love so much. Or I could make pancakes."

"Definitely pancakes," Maggie agreed, adding, "I will need my strength. They plan to take me to a bridal shop."

He leaned forward and kissed her. "I can't wait to have you as my wife."

She considered him thoughtfully. "You've been saying that a lot."

"Not too much, I hope."

Maggie slid her arms about his neck. "That would be impossible. I can't wait to have you as my husband. Is something wrong? You've been acting strange for a few days now."

"I'm a strange man," Dillon explained with a mischievous leer, hoping his guilt wasn't obvious. Why did he feel that surprising Maggie was a negative when the others didn't?

"Yes, you are," she agreed with a huge grin. "But you're being stranger than usual."

"Now, should my future bride talk that way about her beloved?"

"Sweetheart, only your future bride can talk that way about her man."

"You gonna go mama bear on anyone who talks bad about me?" Dillon teased.

"And how would you feel about that?"

He shrugged. "It's okay. As long as I get to do the same. Maggie, how do you feel about surprises?"

"I'm all for them. What did you have in mind?"

"It would hardly be a surprise if I told you."

"True. At least give me a clue. What's it for?"

"Our wedding," Dillon responded truthfully.

"Something outrageous and shocking, I hope."

"Do you mean that?" he asked somewhat doubtfully.

She laughed. "I doubt either of us could come up with outrageous or shocking. We're too practical for our own good."

Your friends can, Dillon thought. *Prepare for the surprise of your life, Miss Maggie.*

&

"Dillon's acting strange," Maggie told Mari when she called later that evening.

"How so?"

"I can't put my finger on it exactly. You don't think he's getting cold feet, do you?"

"No way. That man's so eager to marry you. I'm surprised he's waited this long."

"He seems withdrawn. Almost as though he's keeping secrets. I suppose he could be. He did ask if I liked surprises."

"And you told him you do, I hope?"

"I did."

"What do you think is on his mind?" Mari prompted.

"For one thing, he doesn't want to be a foster parent."

"Did he say that?"

"Not in so many words, but he keeps saying he wants couple time."

"Makes sense. The more people in the mix, the more confusing it becomes," Mari pointed out.

"I feel like I'm letting the program down."

"You didn't plan on falling in love, Maggie. Does that mean you should give up your own happiness for the sake of the foster children?"

"No. . .but you know what I mean."

"They'll understand once you explain you're getting married and your future husband wants you to himself for a while."

"They did," Maggie said. "I've already told the caseworker. She said she'd keep me in mind until the wedding, but I haven't heard from them. I enjoyed Marsha and looked forward to working with other children. I don't know why it didn't occur to me sooner."

"It wasn't God's plan."

"True. How are the kids? It's been a while since I've seen them."

"They miss you. Luke asked to go see Miss Maggie earlier. Right after I told him to pick up his toys."

Maggie laughed. "That's one wise kid you have there."

"Too wise for his own good. It's all I can do to stay two steps ahead of him. Thankfully the others are nothing like Luke."

"Give them time. With a brother like him, I'm sure they'll soon learn."

"Gee, Maggie, thanks for brightening my day."

"You know you love it."

"I do. My children are as precious to me as we are to God."

"I love being a child of God," Maggie agreed.

"Me, too. I'd better go. Matt's yelling at the twins. Don't forget, we're going to the bridal shop tomorrow."

"It's a waste of time."

"Come on, Maggie, be a sport. Joe's taking care of the kids so I can have the day off. You wouldn't deprive me of that, would you?"

"Never."

&

"You're looking particularly beautiful this morning," Dillon said after Maggie kissed him.

The heavenly smell of the pancakes made Maggie's mouth water. "You know this is going straight to my hips, don't you?"

"A few pancakes never hurt anyone."

"I don't have your metabolism."

He handed her a plate. "We could take long walks on the beach every morning."

Maggie settled at the table, shaking out her napkin. "That's difficult with my shifts. You'd think all that walking the floors would help, but it doesn't."

After they said grace, she cut off a bite of pancake and forked it into her mouth.

"You could always quit your job," Dillon said.

She took a sharp, deep breath. "You don't quit, do you?"

He stared wordlessly.

"You're changing everything," Maggie declared stubbornly. She could see from his shocked expression that she'd come at him out of left field with this one. "Slowly easing me from my life. Your place for mine. . ."

"We can live in your house," Dillon interrupted. "I just thought Mom's place would give us more space."

"There you go with the logic. Who wouldn't want a bigger house? To retire at fifty? To travel the world? You're changing my life."

"Mine, too," Dillon defended as he turned away and scraped a burned pancake off the griddle.

"Because you chose to change," Maggie pointed out.

"Okay, if you don't want these things, tell me," Dillon all but shouted, flinging the spatula at the sink. It clattered against the stainless steel interior.

She regretted making him angry. "That's the problem. I do," she admitted in a tiny voice.

Dillon sat down next to her. "What's going on, Maggie?"

"I'm scared."

He reached for her hand. "Why?"

"Of what happens when things get too good. I dreamed of early retirement, but that's all it was—a dream. There's no way I could afford not to work. And now you've proposed that I'll not only retire early but travel, as well. This is a fairy tale, Dillon. Not real life."

"You know I'd never hurt you."

"Maybe not intentionally, but we can't promise it'll never happen. Couples argue."

•

"Is that what we're doing? Arguing?"

"I'm trying to tell you how I feel," she declared, irritation changing her tone. "You've veered so far from that man who thought I was out to cheat your mom."

"I said I was sorry."

"I don't want apologies, Dillon. I need you to understand that sometimes I don't know how to accept the good. There's too much pessimism in me to believe nothing bad will happen."

"If I'd known asking you to quit work would set you off like this, I would have kept my mouth shut."

She rested her hands on his arms. "Oh, Dillon, I should have told you how bad I can get."

"You're not bad, Maggie. And maybe it's past time some good came into your life. I'm not saying you have to quit work, but if you felt inclined, I'd love to have you at home with me."

"I'm so overwhelmed."

His worried expression made her feel even worse. She'd allowed her insecurities to burden them both. "I do want to marry you," she shared quickly. "But remember, I've steered my own course for years."

"And it's going to be difficult to allow someone else to chart changes in the map?"

"Exactly."

"I don't plan to sink your ship, honey. Maybe help steer you around a few obstacles."

"I've provided for myself since I was eighteen years old. The Floyds paid for my education, but I worked to pay for my incidentals. I can't imagine not working. What would I do all day?"

"Whatever you want. Watch the sunrise. Sleep in. Enjoy the sand between your toes. Spend hours listening to the ocean roar. You could help with my handyman project. Wouldn't it be nice to do whatever we want and not have to rush back home so you can go to work?"

"Well yes," Maggie admitted, feeling calmer than before. "I'm not arguing that point."

"So it's fear of change?"

Maggie nodded slowly. "You must think I'm crazy."

"You scared me."

"I don't usually act this way. Maybe it's this outing with the girls that has me acting batty."

"You don't want to go?"

"I do. I don't know what to expect."

"They can't force you to do anything you don't want to do."

Maggie laughed. "Maybe I want to do it all, but I'm afraid to take the leap."

Dillon wrapped his arms about her. "Jump, darling. I promise to catch you. Think of it in terms of being a Christian. We try to offer God advice, but things always go His way, in His time, particularly when we place our faith in Him."

It was the perfect analogy for her. She'd struggled with God's plans for her, too.

"Don't stress so much. As long as we're flexible and communicate, we'll be okay."

Maggie gazed into his eyes. "You promise to love me even when I'm crazy?"

"What choice do I have?" he asked, leaning forward to kiss her.

A horn blew. "Gotta go." Maggie hugged him one last time, forked another bite of pancakes into her mouth, and ran out the door.

"Call me when you get home," Dillon called. "I want to hear about this dress."

"No way," she called back to him.

Dillon dropped into the chair and thought about what had just transpired. Maggie Gregory kept him on an emotional roller coaster. Her reaction to his suggestion had been startling. Was he doing the right thing by keeping her friends' secrets? He wished he knew. Maybe Joe could offer some insight into the situation.

He phoned the church and learned Joe was at home. He called his minister and friend and asked if he had a few minutes to talk. Joe told him to come over.

"Hi, Dillon, come in," Joe invited, closing the front door behind them. "What can I do for you?"

"I wanted to discuss the ladies' plans. I'm not comfortable with the surprise element."

The patter of children's feet sounded down the hall. "Ready, Daddy," Luke announced. When he saw their guest, he shouted, "Hey, Mr. Dillon!" Then he turned around and bellowed, "Mr. Dillon is here."

"Hey, Luke," he said, returning the child's hug when he wrapped his arms about his lower body. Turning to Joe, he said, "I can come back. You're busy."

"We're going outside to play. Come on. We'll talk."

The children ran for the swings and sandboxes, and Joe took a seat on the patio, inviting Dillon to do the same. "Haven't you ever surprised Maggie with something?"

"Her ring when I proposed." And his suggestion she quit work. Dillon didn't mention that. Her reaction had surprised them both. He still didn't understand why it had blown up in his face.

"And you didn't consider it wrong to surprise her with the proposal?"

He shrugged, shaking his head, "No."

"Consider this. God gifted Maggie with a good man and good friends who want to gift her with the perfect wedding."

"There's something else," Dillon offered almost tentatively. "Maggie's foster parenting. She assumes it's a given we will continue to foster children. Our marriage necessitates another review process. I don't have anything to hide, but I have mixed feelings. I never imagined I'd find the love of my life, and I'm not thrilled about sharing her with kids."

"Have you told her?"

He shrugged and nodded. "I shared my doubts. I want to spend time with her. Am I being selfish?"

"I can't answer that, Dillon. Is there another reason you're hesitant? Maggie's only had one foster child, and it went well."

"She was devastated when Marsha went home," Dillon told Joe. "I'm afraid that would happen with every child she brings into her life."

"Maggie would learn to protect her heart with time. Letting go becomes easier with practice. Is that the only reason, Dillon? You don't like seeing Maggie hurt?"

He nodded. "I wish like crazy that we'd met when we were younger and she could have a family of her own. Maggie needs to feel grounded. I'm afraid that denying her foster parenting will take away that outlet for the love she needs to share. I said we could look at it again in a year or so, but neither of us is getting any younger."

"Pray over it."

"I have. Believe me. I'm waiting on God's answer."

"And He will provide. Just let Him guide you both."

fifteen

"And why is it you want to go to the bridal shop?" Maggie asked her friends when they immediately suggested the store. "You know I plan to wear a suit."

"They sell suits," Julie said. "Just dressier than the department stores. You can't have a Plain Jane wedding. There has to be more bling than that ring on your finger."

"So I'll get silver shoes," Maggie countered. "Or maybe white with sparkles."

"You have to try on dresses," Kim insisted. "We plan to live vicariously through you today."

"I'm buying a suit."

Her determined response made Mari ask, "Why are you afraid to try on wedding dresses?" Maggie didn't answer.

"You think you'll want a big wedding if you do," Kim guessed.

"It's not what Dillon wants," Maggie told them. "We agreed to keep it simple."

"It doesn't hurt to look," Julie said. "Wait until you see all those beautiful gowns. You need to try on at least a dozen just because you're the bride-to-be and you can."

Maggie frowned. She hated trying on clothes. "I learned a long time ago not to want what I can't have."

"I don't get it, Maggie. Why can't you have a wedding dress?" Julie asked.

"I'd look silly."

"Because you're fifty?"

"I'm plain old me. Not a movie star or blushing young bride."

"Surely you don't believe any member of Cornerstone would feel you don't deserve a beautiful gown or a fancy wedding because you're an older woman?" Julie asked.

136

"No, but Dillon and I agreed on simple."

"Simple can be many things," Julie pointed out. "My wedding was simple but beautiful. Dillon doesn't care about the wedding. He cares about you being happy."

"Humor us for a couple of hours," Mari suggested, taking her arm and leading her inside. "Then we'll take you to lunch."

Maggie sighed and relented, "Oh, okay, lead on. Let's find the most expensive gowns in the place."

Julie grinned and said, "Now that's the right attitude." Inside, they waited in the upscale showroom, and everyone laughed when Maggie mentioned the television sitcom where two friends dressed in borrowed gowns and pretended to be brides, tossing bouquets back and forth.

"I don't think we'd better try that here," Mari whispered. A well-dressed woman came over and introduced herself as the owner. "Which of you lovely ladies is our bride?"

Maggie felt her skin grow warm when her friends pointed in her direction.

"Congratulations. When's the wedding?"

"The Sunday before Valentine's Day."

The woman nodded. "What did you have in mind?"

"A simple white suit."

"But she wants to try on gowns first," Julie said. "Right, Maggie?"

"My friends insist I have to try on wedding gowns though they know my plans are very simple."

"There are gowns that would be glorious on you," the woman offered, switching into salesperson mode. "Let me show you."

When Maggie stepped up on to the dais wearing the first gown, she had to admit the owner knew what suited her. She felt like a fairy princess wearing a satin halter dress with a tulle skirt and beaded Alençon lace.

The next dress was a satin ball gown adorned with back buttons and a long train detailed with lace appliqué cutouts.

She tried on dress after dress as each of her friends chose their favorite. Then Maggie tried on the dress she'd picked, and they all sighed in delight.

The satin floor-length halter gown with the side drape and flower detail was a perfect fit. The woman produced a long tulle veil that trailed along behind Maggie.

"So what do you think?" Maggie asked as she pirouetted before the mirror and looked over her shoulder at the back of the gown. They all agreed she should choose this one.

She took one more look and remembered her intent. No matter how she felt in the dress, it wasn't part of her plans. "I don't know why I let them talk me into this," she told the owner. "Do you have white suits?"

"Of course. I'll bring a couple into the dressing room."

"Maggie, wait!" Julie cried, stepping up on the dais next to her. "Don't you think she should choose this one?" she asked the owner.

"It suits her, but if she doesn't want the gown, then we'll find her what she wants."

"But it's perfect. It doesn't even need alterations. Even the length is exactly right."

"Julie, please," Maggie requested softly. "Don't make me want this more than I already do."

"Okay," her friend agreed with a heavy sigh. "Pick out your suit, but I'm paying."

They all knew better than to argue with Julie when she got into this mood. Maggie stepped into the dressing room and removed the dress with Mari's help.

"Julie's disappointed."

Mari looked up from undoing the buttons and nodded at Maggie in the mirror. "She only wants you to have a beautiful dress. We all do."

Her friend came into the dressing room. "Here, try this one," Julie said, handing her a very feminine white lace suit with satin lapels.

The owner brought a knee-length raw silk suit in white

and one with a long skirt, but Maggie chose the one Julie had picked. After the decision was made, the owner called in her seamstress to take Maggie's measurements.

On their way out, a display caught Maggie's eye. She paused to finger the gorgeous lilac dress and sighed in delight. The dress featured the same halter-top style as the wedding dress she'd loved. "If I were having attendants, this is the dress I'd choose."

"We could wear the dresses and serve as honorary attendants," Natalie suggested.

"And you'd know we wanted to be up front with you," Julie agreed.

"It's not practical," Maggie said with a shake of her head. "We'd freeze with our shoulders out in February."

"Ready for lunch?" Natalie asked. "I'm starving."

Maggie agreed. The couple of bites she'd managed that morning had long since left her.

"Thanks again for your help," she told the owner.

"My pleasure. You'll make a beautiful bride."

They were in the car when Julie cried, "I forgot to pay for your dress. Noah says I'd forget my head," she muttered. "Everyone stay put. I'll be right back."

"You really should let me pay for it," Maggie insisted one final time.

"You'll hurt my feelings if you don't let me give you this gift."

Maggie couldn't help but wonder why Julie was so adamant. She hadn't insisted on giving Kim her dress. But then Kim's parents had paid for her wedding. And Julie and Mari had worn the same gown for their weddings. Maybe it was because Maggie didn't have a family.

Julie was gone for several minutes and grinned like a Cheshire cat when she crawled into the backseat with Natalie and Kim and said, "Mission accomplished."

At their favorite restaurant, Mari took Maggie's arm and led her inside while the others removed packages from the trunk.

"What are they doing?" she asked, glancing back over her shoulder.

"You'll see." They followed the hostess to a small private room in the rear of the restaurant. The others arrived, stacking their packages on a nearby table.

"Okay, give," Maggie demanded, her gaze shifting from face to face.

"Welcome to your shower," Kim said.

"That's right, practical one," Julie said, "even if you act like Scrooge over the wedding, we're giving you a shower. We decided not to embarrass you by having this particular event at church, but there are a few necessities every new bride must have."

Maggie groaned. "You'll be the death of me yet, Julie Loughlin."

Everyone chuckled and reached for their menus. After choosing their entrées, they enjoyed their iced tea and the blooming onion appetizer Natalie ordered.

"So what did you think about the gowns?" Mari asked.

"They were all beautiful. That one would have been perfect if we were having a formal wedding. But the suit serves the purpose, and I can wear it again."

"What would your dream wedding be like?" Kim asked.

"Marrying Dillon is a dream for me. I never expected to fall in love with him."

"Not after the way he treated you when you first met," Kim said.

Kim had been her faithful defender when it came to Dillon's treatment of her. "Dillon feels guilty that he allowed strangers to care for Mrs. Allene. He knows I loved her like a mother."

"And wishes she could be here for the wedding?" Mari asked.

"Yes. And my parents, of course. They've been dead for years, but I miss them still."

"You always will," Mari said, her eyes tearing up. She, too, had lost her mother. Julie reached over to squeeze her sister-in-law's hand.

"I'm sorry," Maggie whispered. "I didn't mean to upset you."

"You didn't," Mari said with a gentle smile. "I was blessed to have my mother sitting in the front pew when I married Joe. You, Joe, and Julie weren't as fortunate."

"I need to call Mom tonight," Kim said with a sheepish look.

"Let me tell you what Dillon said this morning," Maggie said, steering the conversation to a happier subject.

"That he loves you?" Julie asked.

Surprised, Maggie said, "Yes. He says that all the time lately."

Julie shrugged. "All men in love should say it often. So what did he say?"

"He suggested I retire."

Everyone looked startled.

"And what did you say?" Julie demanded.

Maggie looked embarrassed. "I accused him of trying to change everything about my life. He thinks I'm crazy."

"I doubt that," Mari comforted. "Is early retirement something you'd consider?"

"He says he doesn't want to sit around for long days waiting for me to get off work and that he can afford to support us both."

"You'd be crazy to say no," Julie said.

"He keeps knocking my feet out from under me with these surprises," Maggie explained. "Helping with the house, the proposal, this ring, and now this."

"Sounds as if he's smitten," Julie declared.

Maggie nodded, and everyone laughed.

"You deserve to be loved, and now that we know Dillon better, we know he's the man for you," Mari said.

"I hope I'm the woman for him."

"Don't ever doubt it, Maggie Gregory," Julie said sternly. "Dillon Rogers is the lucky one. Not every man has you in his life, and don't ever let him forget it."

"That's right," Kim agreed. "Our husbands are blessed to have us as their wives, and now that you're about to get married, we're going to find Natalie her Mr. Right."

"Oh, Lord, deliver me," Natalie said, raising her gaze heavenward in supplication.

After their meal, they ordered dessert and lingered over the bridal shower.

"This is for your wedding night," Mari said, passing Maggie a beautifully wrapped package.

Maggie opened the box to find a virginal white satin night-gown and matching robe—the nightwear a mother often gave her daughter. Tears welled in her eyes as she considered Mari's thoughtfulness. "Thank you."

"And these go with that," Julie said with a teasing grin, passing her what appeared to be a shoe box.

Inside, Maggie found a pair of white satin and marabou slippers with three-inch heels. "I'll break my neck."

"But just think, when you fall, Dillon will be there to catch you."

The laughter started and didn't stop as Maggie opened box after box.

"It's only a matter of time before you're wearing one of Dillon's old T-shirts and sleeping in drawstring pajama pants again," Kim said, handing Maggie another box. "You won't be able to help yourself. They're just too comfortable. But if there's a time when you need to remind Dillon you're all woman, this should do the trick."

Almost afraid to open the box, Maggie found a short red satin nightie inside.

"Wow," Julie said.

Maggie adored the romantic garments she would have never bought for herself. "This is too much," she declared tearfully.

"It's never too much for our friend," they said.

Julie lifted her tea glass into the air. "To Maggie."

"To Maggie," they repeated in unison.

❧

"Are you having second thoughts?" Maggie asked Dillon later that night after she told him about the trip to the bridal shop and the surprise shower. Was it her imagination, or did he seem to withdraw with the question?

"Why would you ask that?"

"Well, after my attack this morning, I wouldn't be surprised if you were reconsidering. And I can't put my finger on it, but you're different somehow."

Dillon slipped his arm about her and pulled her against his chest. "I'm thinking about counseling and being a good husband, but I'm not about to change my mind. February can't get here fast enough."

She smiled at him. "I started sorting through some stuff that I'll probably give away."

"You don't have to do that. We'll find a place for everything."

"We should talk about what we want to keep for our place."

"Your sofa is more comfortable than Mom's," Dillon said, settling further into the deep sofa.

"We could flip-flop pieces and rent the house furnished."

"Or donate them to charity. We're bound to have more than we need."

"Mari could use a new couch. The kids are hard on their furniture."

"I still haven't gone through the attic," Dillon told her. "Let's see if there's anything up there they can use."

"That sounds like a plan."

sixteen

Shopping for her dress and being surprised by her shower had made the approaching nuptials even more real for Maggie. Then Joe Dennis called to set an actual start-up date for their pre-marital counseling. On the first night, Maggie couldn't quiet the butterflies in her stomach as she and Dillon sat with Pastor Joe in his home study.

He closed the door and settled in an old recliner while they sat on the sofa. "It's not often I get to give these sessions one on one," Joe told them. "I'm really glad to have this opportunity to counsel you both. Loving each other is important, but you'll find areas that require negotiation if you want a happy, long-lasting marriage.

"I'll outline the plans for the meetings in a few minutes, but first I want to ask what your biggest concerns are. Maggie, ladies first; what's your major concern about marriage?"

She laughed nervously. "You want me to pick just one?" When Joe nodded, she said, "Fear."

He shrugged. "Define 'fear.'"

She wrung her hands. "That I won't be the wife Dillon deserves."

"We've discussed that," Dillon objected. "I have no expectations."

"And you feel that's realistic?" Joe asked.

Perplexed, Dillon glanced at Maggie and back at Joe. "I feel we can work things out as we go. That's the way we've handled things so far."

"Have you considered that continuing to do it that way will put unnecessary stress on your marriage?"

Dillon's brows drew together. "How so?"

"What side of the bed do you prefer?"

"The left."

"You, Maggie?"

"The left."

"Only one left side of the bed." They looked at each other. "So someone has to take the right side. How do you decide? Does one of you opt to be the bigger person and make the sacrifice? Do you flip a coin? Does the one who gets there first get the left side? Or will you discuss it and come to an agreement that works best for you both?"

"I suppose we'll discuss it," Dillon said.

"I know it seems simple, but it's just the beginning. You'll agree to accept things about each other, little things that drive you crazy and can cause major problems if you're not prepared to handle them. What about you, Dillon? What's your biggest issue?"

He looked at her. "I'm not sure Maggie trusts me to do what's best for her."

"Trust is important," Joe agreed. "Do you trust Dillon, Maggie?"

She nodded. "I wouldn't have said yes to your proposal if I didn't believe you love me."

"But do you trust him?" Joe repeated. "Do you feel you can put your life in his hands and know he'll take care of you?"

"I hadn't considered that marriage was turning yourself over to another person and depending on them to take care of you. I think of it as a partnership—both of us looking out for each other."

"What about Dillon being the Christian head of your household? Him making decisions that you might not wholeheartedly agree with?"

"I've made my own decisions for years, and I'm not likely to stop once we're married."

"I don't plan to take over her life."

"But you will," Joe said. "You say you don't have expectations, but you do. You expect Maggie to trust you to do the right thing. How can you know what the right thing is if you don't discuss it?"

"I don't think we need to talk every little thing to death," Dillon objected.

Joe rested his chin on steepled fingers and said, "I can see you're already uncomfortable, but these sessions are intended to help you grow as a couple. We may move out of your comfort zones, but please don't shut down on me."

They nodded, and Joe asked, "Do you need to communicate?"

"Sure," Dillon agreed. "I can't understand what she wants if she doesn't tell when I ask."

"Does she have to wait until you ask?"

He frowned. "No. Maggie's not a game player, and I like that."

"I know you had issues with her when you first met and that you've resolved them. Do you feel guilty for the way you treated her?"

"I've apologized, and she's accepted my apologies. But yes, I do feel guilty."

"What about forgive and forget? Maybe Maggie doesn't want you to bring that up anymore. She wants to forget it ever happened."

"Is that true?" Dillon asked. "Did you tell him that?"

"No," she defended, looking at Pastor Joe with surprise. "I can't really tell anyone how I feel."

"Not even me?" he asked, sounding disappointed.

"Not even me," she countered. "I have issues from the past, Dillon. Things that will affect our marriage more than I'd like."

"Maggie hasn't shared anything with me, Dillon, but look at how easily you made an assumption that she had."

"I'm sorry."

"You allowed a communication you heard to affect your thought processes. Rather than thinking it over, you reacted, and that knee-jerk reaction can sometimes haunt your marriage forever. Once words leave your lips, you can't pull them back. And regardless of how the old saying goes, words can hurt."

Once more, both Maggie and Dillon nodded.

"Here's how I'd like to proceed. We have six weeks until the wedding. In the past, I've done four-, six-, and even eight-week sessions, depending on the couple."

"And one week," Maggie said, reminding him of Julie and Noah.

"If I hadn't already known my sister and Noah so well, I'd never have allowed that," Joe said. "Anyway, I believe we can do this in four weeks. Tonight, I want you to complete a test. You need to answer the questions without discussing them with each other. We'll discuss the answers as we go into our sessions."

The room grew quiet as Joe gave them each a clipboard and suggested Dillon move to his chair.

"There are no right or wrong answers. Just questions that will provoke you to consider a number of pertinent points that relate to marriage. If you have any questions, ask. I'll be glad to help. Mari baked cookies today. You get started, and I'll get our refreshments."

Occasionally, Maggie glanced up to find Dillon looking thoughtful. She wondered where he was on the questionnaire. And while she knew the answers were supposed to be her own, she couldn't help but wonder how he had responded.

Later the mood was contemplative as they walked toward home.

"That test was something else," Dillon said.

It had been rather eye opening, Maggie thought. "Amazing how many things we never really considered."

"Like preferring the same side of the bed?" When Maggie nodded, he assured her, "That's not really a problem."

"Something else you'll give up for me?"

He reached for her hand. "You'd do the same for me. I can see where counseling will be beneficial. And just because we're not always in full agreement over everything doesn't mean things can't work out. That's where compromise comes into play. I think we're pretty good at that."

Are we? Maggie wondered. How many times had she gone along with Dillon's decisions? What other differences would the test answers reveal?

"Come look at the ceiling. I finished it today. I'll make you a berry smoothie."

Maggie loved the fruity taste of the smoothies Dillon blended for her. He'd started keeping ingredients on hand and sometimes brought supplies to her house, as well.

"I want to know how you answered those questions on bank accounts," she said as he let them into the house.

Maggie admired the ceiling and sat at the kitchen island while Dillon whirled ingredients in the blender. "Did you take the shirt back yet?" she asked. She'd given him the shirt for Christmas and had guessed at his size. She didn't think he liked the shirt but knew he'd keep it for fear of hurting her feelings by taking it back.

"No. It's okay."

"It's too big," Maggie argued. "Give it to me. I'll exchange it for a smaller size."

"I'll handle it," he promised. "You already have enough to do."

"Exchange it for something you like. I don't mind," she said.

"I used my new woodworking tools yesterday. I can't believe how long I looked and waited to buy them. Now I have several projects in mind."

It pleased her that she'd found something he liked.

"How's the new purse working out?"

Dillon had given her a very expensive handbag, and while Maggie wasn't thrilled with the various compartments, she carried it daily. Soon she'd fill him in on how personal the preference for handbags really was. "Good. The girls at work love it."

He slid a glass on the island before her and shuffled through the drawer.

"What are you looking for?"

"I found something for you at the grocery store. I'm positive I stuck them in here," he muttered. "Ah, here they are."

Maggie laughed when he handed her a straw with a spoon on the end.

"How's this for when your smoothie is too thick to drink?"

Maggie trailed her fingers along his jaw. "You're a keeper, Dillon Rogers."

He sat on the stool next to her, his hands cradling her face as he kissed her. "No matter what the test results say?"

"It's not a test," Maggie said. "More of a 'getting to know you' tool."

"Like those icebreaker things at meetings?"

"Exactly. And I look forward to learning everything about my future husband."

"And changing the parts you don't like?" he asked.

Maggie shook her head. "No. We accept those things and celebrate our differences."

"I can't tell you how much I appreciate hearing that from you."

"They're not just words, Dillon. I'll respect your role as head of our home, but I expect you to communicate with me."

"I do."

"Yeah, like that plant list Keith Harris sent me. I thought you promised to let me make the decisions about my house."

"I did. But if you look, you'll find everything is the same as what you had in your yard before."

"I saw a couple of hundred dollars in flowers."

He quickly swallowed the sip of smoothie and said, "Those were for here."

"My future home, you mean?"

"I know you love flowers, and I thought I'd have him bring a few things over."

"I'd rather go to the nursery and pick them out myself. I go every spring to choose what I put in my planters and add to my landscaping. Your beds are full of bulbs. Haven't you noticed the crocuses and daffodils pushing through?"

"You'll have to show me."

"Don't you garden?" It was high on Maggie's retirement list. She looked forward to spending more time in her yard.

He shrugged. "Until this summer, I hadn't used a lawn mower since I was a teenager."

"Your life has been so different."

They finished their smoothies, and Maggie took the glasses over to the sink. She rinsed them and the blender before putting everything in the dishwasher. "So how did you answer those banking questions?"

"I'm flexible. Mom and Dad had a joint account, but if you'd rather keep them separate, that's okay. We could have a household account."

If she took advantage of Dillon's plan for her to retire early, what would she put into the account? Rent money from the house maybe. Possibly a little money from her retirement, but it wouldn't amount to much.

"Did I tell you Natalie might be interested in renting my place?"

"No. That's a great idea."

"We're going to talk about it next week. She'd like a bigger kitchen."

"Hope it works out. It would be nice to have that resolved before our wedding. Definitely before the honeymoon."

"Where are we going?" she asked.

"It's a surprise."

Maggie pushed her hair behind her ears and said, "It'll be an even bigger surprise when you end up going by yourself because I didn't get enough time off from work."

Dillon frowned. "Why won't you just give up your job?"

"Because I have personal expenses that I can't expect you to cover."

"My money will be yours, Maggie."

She didn't want to argue about this again. "Should I ask for a week of vacation? I need to get my request on the books."

"Can you swing two? I have something special in mind."

She sprayed the countertop with a disinfectant spray and used a paper towel to wipe it away. "I'll ask."

seventeen

January slipped away, and the groundhog predicted another six weeks of cold weather. Though cold outside, Maggie felt warmly cocooned in Dillon's love. At least during those times she allowed herself to be happy.

Dillon's determination to make everything special for her showed through in the attention he showered on her. Maggie had never known what being spoiled could be like, but his behavior certainly mirrored what she'd imagined. He took care of her in so many ways. She couldn't begin to count the number of times she'd come home to prepared meals or they had dined out when she was tired after work. He'd even offered to run errands when she so much as mentioned a need.

The counseling sessions were going better than she'd thought. Joe had expertly talked them through the few things they disagreed on, including foster care. Maggie hadn't been surprised to learn Dillon's main objection had to do with her being hurt when the children went away. And she'd made the decision to give him the couple time he needed.

They discussed Dillon's love of travel and Maggie's admitted preference for home. When Joe asked why, she could only admit how much she had always considered home the place where she belonged.

Both Dillon and Joe had impressed upon her that home wasn't always a building.

"What if Dillon had to go back to Saudi?" Joe asked. "Would you let him go rather than give up your home and friends here?"

Maggie shrugged. "I wouldn't want to. But I can't say what I'd do, and truthfully I'm thankful I don't have to make the decision."

"But it's always a possibility. When Mari and I married, I'm sure she thought we'd remain in Colorado. Our lives changed, but she was willing to follow me." He picked up his Bible and flipped through the tissuelike pages.

"In Ruth 1:16, we read 'Intreat me not to leave thee, or to return from following after thee: for whither thou goest, I will go; and where thou lodgest, I will lodge: thy people shall be my people, and thy God my God.' When you marry, this becomes your promise to each other," Joe said.

"And I will promise that," Maggie said, glancing at Dillon as she spoke. "I just know I need roots. And I need Dillon to understand why home is so important to me." To her dismay, her voice broke slightly.

Dillon reached for her hand. "And I'm trying, Maggie. But you have to move forward with me. I want nothing for you but happiness."

"I suspect Maggie's nomadic existence in her childhood has a great deal to do with her need for a home," Joe offered. "You did say you lived in a number of foster homes after your father's death."

Maggie nodded.

"You stayed with the Floyds the longest. Why not remain in Virginia?"

"A college friend grew up in Myrtle Beach. She brought me here for a visit once, and I fell in love with the area. After Mr. Floyd retired and they began to travel, I decided to make the move. Sometimes I think God orchestrated it so I'd come here and find Him."

"And me," Dillon offered. "I've been studying my Bible, too, praying for scripture that would bring you comfort," he told her. "I ran across Psalm 90:1 last night. 'Lord, thou hast been our dwelling place in all generations.'"

"Very good, Dillon," Joe agreed. "There's no more perfect dwelling place than in the Lord."

"I understand what you're saying," Maggie told them. "And I want to feel that way. Truly I do."

"We'll pray over this," Joe promised. "Your happiness is in God and the love He's given you. Not in a place."

ॐ

On Tuesday night, Dillon had a church meeting, and Natalie called to invite Maggie out to dinner at their favorite restaurant.

"So what have you been up to lately?" Maggie asked.

"Avery and I are working together on a special cake."

That surprised Maggie. "What kind of cake?"

"For Love Day."

"What's that? A Valentine celebration?" she asked curiously, surprised no one had mentioned the event to her. Natalie nodded and concentrated on adding dressing to her salad. "Why didn't anyone tell me? I would have helped."

"You've been busy with your counseling sessions."

"Not too busy to help out at church," Maggie protested.

"It's no big deal, Maggie. You do a lot for Cornerstone. Give others an opportunity to do their part."

"I suppose the bigger deal is that you and Avery are actually working together. How did you manage that?"

Natalie shrugged. "Same committee assignment. I think Avery agreed so he could get my cake batter recipe."

Maggie laughed. "That sounds paranoid."

"I gave it to him."

Maggie's head shot up, and she stared at her friend. "You did?"

"Sure. The biggest thing about my cakes is originality. I know what combinations taste good together and what makes them pretty. Believe me, it's not just the cake alone."

"Whatever it is, it's delicious. What do you think about making a cake to serve at the after-church fellowship on our wedding day?"

"I could do that."

"On second thought, I'm not so sure it's a great idea," Maggie said. "We're already holding people up from their Sunday lunch. How do you think they'd feel about a sugar high on top of that?"

"They're going to stay and wish you well anyway. And you've seen how they gobble up the cookies and coffee. What did you have in mind?"

"My favorite is chocolate, and Dillon likes orange. Surprise us."

Natalie nodded. "How is counseling going?"

Maggie sipped her tea. "Good. I didn't realize it would be so involved, but we worked through some things, and I think our marriage will be stronger because of that."

"You said 'think.' Are you still having doubts?"

Maggie sighed and nodded. "Never about Dillon."

"Don't let the past stand in the way of your future," Natalie advised. "Remember a few weeks back when Pastor Joe spoke on God forgiving our sins? Doubting yourself doesn't make you a good Christian, nor will it make you a good wife."

"I love Dillon. I thank God for him all the time. Still, I can't go along with every suggestion he makes and feel comfortable."

"Like what?"

"Giving up my job. I have expenses. I don't feel right about letting him pay them. And it doesn't seem fair for him to support our home solely with his income."

"That comes from being a sole provider for so long. You're used to doing for yourself, but you have to accept that Dillon needs to take care of you, too."

"But how do I take care of him?"

Natalie grinned at Maggie. "My mom sat me down years ago and told me how to keep a man. Plain and simple, you love him. That's all he wants from you.

"Mom said men see themselves as providers. That's how it works, and divorce happens when two people can't communicate their needs to each other."

"It's good advice," Maggie agreed. "I've been praying that God would help me."

"I think we need to get together and pray for you like we did for Kim."

"I wouldn't mind. It's been awhile."

"Let's do it then. Is Dillon having a bachelor party?"

"I don't think so."

"Maybe Wyatt and Joe can plan something for him, and we can have a bachelorette party. I'll call everyone."

"It doesn't have to be about my wedding," Maggie protested.

"We love you, Maggie. But God loves you more. He sent you Dillon. He will equip you to become the wife you need to be."

⋙

"We got our marriage license today," Maggie announced as they settled in Kim's living room. "This wedding is really going to happen."

"Did you doubt it?" Mari asked.

Maggie glanced at Natalie then back at Mari. "Natalie told me God will strengthen me, and I believe that. I'm praying hard."

"We're praying, too," Julie assured. "We haven't stopped since we asked God to send you a husband."

"Maggie, you've come a long way in life, and you deserve to be happy," Kim said.

"I know how she feels," Julie said. "I married Noah knowing I wasn't cut out to be a minister's wife, but God makes it work. I love Noah more today than when I married him."

"I feel the same about Wyatt," Kim said. "Every day gets better and better."

"Hey, you're depressing me," Natalie offered with a little laugh. "I wouldn't mind having what you all have."

"Don't worry. It's in God's hands," Mari reassured.

"I've got news to share before I bust," Kim said.

"You're pregnant," Maggie guessed immediately.

Kim radiated her delight. "Wyatt is very happy."

"And so is your mom," Maggie added. "When are they moving back?" Everyone laughed at Maggie's teasing.

"Not to steal Kim's thunder, but I have an announcement myself," Julie said with a wide grin.

"You, too?" Maggie asked. When Julie nodded, Maggie glanced at Mari. "Did you know?"

"I knew Julie thought she might be."

Maggie hugged her friends. "I'm so happy for you both. I can't wait to see your babies. I know they'll be as beautiful as their mothers."

"Thanks, Maggie," Julie said. "You're a good friend. You deserve all the happiness God has in store for you."

eighteen

"Shouldn't you be getting dressed for a wedding?"

Maggie glanced at Julie and smiled. "It won't take me long to change."

"You're not nervous?"

Maggie shrugged. "I have a few jitters."

"Then you're blessed. I'm sure my shakes registered on the Richter scale."

As she laughed at Julie's comment, the nursery room door opened and Joe stepped inside. "Maggie, they had to rush Chester Simpson to the hospital this morning, and I need to go over and be with Geneva. Noah is going to preach the second service. If it's okay, I thought we might do the ceremony at six this evening. Dillon says it's up to you."

A postponement by the pastor. *What next?* Maggie wondered. "We can wait, I suppose."

"Thanks, Maggie. I don't want Geneva to be alone."

"Me, either," Maggie agreed, flashing him a big smile. "Besides, it's not as if you're throwing off a major production."

"Thanks for understanding. Noah could perform the service if you'd rather not wait."

"No." She glanced across the room to where Julie kneeled between two toddlers and looked back at Joe. "No offense to Noah, but I consider you my pastor."

Joe squeezed her hand. "I'm glad. I want to hear you say your vows."

"We'll see you at six then. Tell the Simpsons I'm praying for them."

"Will do," Joe said, waving at his sister as he hurried from the room.

"What's going on?" Julie asked.

Maggie settled a toddler at the table and gave him a toy. "Chester Simpson had to go to the hospital. Joe asked if we could delay the ceremony until this evening."

Julie looked startled. "And you're okay with that?"

"It's fine. Dillon will be my husband, and that's all that matters."

"Um, Maggie, I need to take care of something. I'll be back in a few minutes."

"Take your time. We've got plenty of help this morning."

After church, Mari, Kimberly, Julie, Natalie, and Peg gathered around Maggie. She explained what had happened.

"We're picking you up at four thirty so you can dress here at the church," Kim told her.

"I can put my suit on at home."

"I thought I'd put your hair up," she offered.

"I don't have a veil, so that might be better than wearing it down around my shoulders."

"And I want to do your makeup," Julie said.

"Dillon's not going to recognize me."

"Oh, he's going to know his beautiful bride," Mari declared. "Go home, rest a bit, and take a bubble bath. We'll be there before you know it."

The afternoon sped by. After gathering what she needed for the wedding, Maggie finished packing for their honeymoon. They had decided to leave the next day though Dillon still insisted on keeping his plans a surprise.

As promised, her friends arrived en masse. She got her dress from the bedroom, along with the bag containing her other necessities. "We can walk to the church," Maggie said as she slipped her new shoes on and took a couple of steps. "On second thought, let's drive. I don't know why I let you talk me into these things."

"You'd wear those white nursing clogs if we'd let you," Kim said.

"Flip-flops would have been better if it weren't so cold."

At the church, they ushered her into the room where all

Cornerstone brides dressed for their weddings.

"I need to make sure everything is okay in the sanctuary," Maggie said.

"I'll do it," Mari said, guiding her toward Kim.

Kim pushed a chair up behind Maggie. "Let's do your hair first. What if we pull it up in curls?"

"I'd like that."

Mari returned and pronounced the sanctuary to be in perfect order.

Several minutes later, Kim held up a mirror. "What do you think?"

Maggie touched the mass of curls. "Thanks, Kim. This is so much better than wearing it down."

Julie stepped forward. "Now for the makeup."

"I don't wear much."

"More won't hurt tonight. You're paler than usual."

"In shock from all this attention," Maggie teased.

"It's only just begun," Natalie said.

Maggie looked at her. "What else are you planning?"

"To marry you off to Dillon," Natalie said.

Maggie relaxed and allowed Julie to work on her face. When Julie held up the mirror again, Maggie could hardly believe her eyes. "You're a miracle worker."

"Brides are the best makeover candidates. They glow."

Maggie laughed. "This skin hasn't glowed in years."

"Well, it does now," Kim declared. "Let's get you into your dress, and then we can change."

Confusion filled Maggie when Julie unzipped a second garment bag. "That's not my suit." She stared at the material that flowed from the bag when Julie shifted it out. She immediately recognized her dream dress from the bridal store.

"Oh, honey, please don't cry," Mari said, jerking tissues from a nearby box.

"It is your dress," Julie said. "You looked so beautiful in it. Please don't be upset that I bought it for you."

Maggie looked into their expectant faces and knew there

was no way she could be angry. "You're right. I deserve to be a princess on my wedding day."

"That's the spirit," Julie declared. "Sit down, and let Kim pin the veil in your hair."

Kim put the tulle veil into place and secured it with hairpins.

Maggie looked around at Julie. "What would you have done if I'd said no?"

"Begged and pleaded," Julie said. "And the suit won't be a waste. You can wear it for another formal event."

"I love you all."

"We love you, too," Mari said, hugging her close.

"There's more than the dress, isn't there?" Maggie asked.

The women looked at each other.

"Yes," Mari answered truthfully.

"What have you planned?"

"Every minute detail," Julie said.

"Including Mr. Chester's hospital visit this morning?"

"No. That's was God's intervention," Julie assured. "We struggled to find a way to change the time, and it just happened. And praise God, Mr. Chester only had indigestion and not a heart attack."

Maggie shook her head in disbelief. How could she not love these women? "So what do we do?"

"Just let the ceremony unfold as planned. We did all the stressful worrying for you."

"Does Dillon know?"

"Not everything. Please don't be upset with him, either. We dragged him into our scheme to surprise you. We told him to say he couldn't wait to have you as his wife anytime you acted like you suspected something."

Maggie grinned. "That explains his strange behavior."

"He had his reservations, but he couldn't find anything wrong with doing this for you."

Truthfully, Maggie couldn't either. Knowing her friends loved her enough to make her day extra special meant a lot.

The group of them soon had her in the gown. As they smoothed and tucked, she found it difficult to take her eyes off the bride reflected in the cheval mirror. She had fought this so hard, but Maggie knew this was what she wanted for her wedding. Over the last few days, she'd struggled, reassuring herself the lace suit would be fine, but now she understood what they had tried to tell her.

When they unzipped their garment bags to reveal duplicates of the lilac tea-length gown she'd admired at the bridal shop, Maggie shook her head.

"You did say this was the dress you would have picked," Kim pointed out.

"But I didn't mean you had to buy it. You could have worn something you already had."

"Oh please!" Julie cried. "I didn't want my picture taken on your wedding day wearing some old dress I'd worn a million times."

"I suppose all the guys are wearing tuxedos?"

"You've never seen a more handsome bunch," Kim told her. There was a tap on the door.

"Can we come in and say hello to the bride?"

Maggie gasped at the sight of the Floyds. Though they had stayed in contact by phone, she hadn't seen them in years. She moved to hug them.

"You look stunning," Sharon Floyd declared, taking Maggie's hands in hers.

"I can't believe you're here. I would have invited you, but Dillon and I planned to say our vows after church and didn't think it was practical to ask you to come so far for a fifteen-minute ceremony."

"We're glad your lovely friends planned this beautiful wedding. You deserve it, Maggie."

Mari introduced herself to the Floyds and then looked at Maggie and whispered, "We thought perhaps Mr. and Mrs. Floyd could walk you down the aisle and give you away."

A lump formed in her throat. "I'd love that."

Mari wrapped an arm about Maggie's waist for support. "Wyatt is Dillon's best man. Noah and Avery are groomsmen."

"Avery?"

"Yes," Natalie said. "I'll tell you the story of how we became friends while working together on your cake design."

"Love Day?" Maggie asked.

Natalie nodded. "That's the code name for your wedding."

"I can't wait to hear that story. It sounds as miraculous as mine and Dillon's."

Mari took Maggie's hand in hers. "Just enjoy and accept this gift from the people who love you. You deserve this, Maggie. Now don't cry," she whispered when tears welled in Maggie's eyes. "We can do a lot, but we can't work miracles with red eyes."

Maggie giggled and blinked away the tears. These women were her true sisters.

"Ready?" Julie asked.

"Wait!" Peg cried. "The flowers." She handed each of the women a single purple rose. "These are my contribution. To repay you for your kindness to Chloe and me."

Maggie hugged her.

Natalie pinned corsages on the Floyds. Peg removed the bridal bouquet from its box. "Dillon sent this. There are fifty miniature white rosebuds. Here's the card. He put it in the envelope. No one else read it."

Maggie felt the tears surge again as she read, "Please be happy about this. Your friends had me the moment they said you deserved the best. I agree. I love you. Dillon."

Kim smacked her forehead. "Dillon sent your something old." She shuffled through the items in her bag and pulled out a jewelry box.

Inside, Maggie found Mrs. Allene's pearls and gasped. When she'd suggested he save his mother's jewelry for his wife, she'd never imagined she would fill that role.

"Everyone's waiting," Julie declared as she secured the pearls about Maggie's throat.

Her mouth fell open when the sanctuary doors opened to show the church fully decorated for her Valentine wedding. Candles, greenery, and two tall vases of red roses rested on the pulpit. More candles gleamed in the dark windows. Kim's white ribbons decorated the pews.

Maggie's gaze focused on the Good Shepherd window. Jesus held out His hand, encouraging her to take that first step. She had never felt the presence of the Lord more fully in her life than at this particular moment.

Her attendants started down the aisle.

"When did you have time?" she asked as Mari adjusted the veil.

"It started the day you told us what you planned, and it just snowballed. We had a meeting at church, and your wedding became Project Love Day. I think every member of the church has been here at one time or another this afternoon. You have a ton of thank-you cards to write."

Too choked up to speak, Maggie nodded.

"Maggie, look at me!" Marsha cried, twirling in the beautifully embroidered white and lavender junior bridesmaid's dress.

"You're beautiful, honey." Tears welled in Maggie's eyes. If she made it through this wedding without looking like a raccoon, it would be a miracle.

Luke stood nearby holding her ring pillow with pride.

"Thank you," she whispered to Mari.

"No more tears," Mari ordered. "This is a joyous day."

Very much so. Maggie had not known such joy since her parents died. This was exactly the type of wedding she would have chosen if they'd been alive.

"Ready?" Mr. Floyd asked, patting her hand when it trembled against his arm.

When her gaze shifted to Dillon, the love in his expression stole her breath away. He looked very handsome in his black tails.

Love more encompassing than she'd ever known came over

her. The love of Jesus—Maggie was sure of that. All those years she'd felt so alone, God had cared. Before she'd ever known Him as her Savior, He'd known and loved her.

He had given her parents to replace those she'd lost, friends to enrich her life, and the man she loved with all her heart. And He'd given her another family—that of God. Nothing could make this day better.

Mari kissed her cheek. "See you down front." She whispered directions to the children before she walked in carefully measured steps toward the front.

This is so surreal, Maggie thought as she waited. And then it was her turn. The music changed and everyone stood as she took her first step. She felt like a princess as she heard the soft gasps of several women in the audience.

Maggie nearly cried again when Joe asked who gave this woman to be married and Mr. Floyd pronounced, "We do, in her parents' honor." Her focus never left Dillon as they spoke their vows.

"I present to you Mr. and Mrs. Aaron Dillon Rogers. You may kiss your bride."

Applause filled the church as Dillon kissed her for the first time as her husband.

"Ready?" he asked, taking her arm and heading toward the exit.

In the background, Maggie heard Joe announce, "The reception will be held in the church fellowship hall."

"Pictures first," Julie declared when they exited the front doors. They returned to the front of the church and went through the formal poses.

Maggie held Dillon's hand. "I can't believe this is real."

"Quite a leap from that simple service we planned."

"Do you mind?"

Dillon raised her hand to his lips. The camera flashed. "All I wanted was you as my wife. I didn't care how we got there. I had reservations when they started talking about surprising you. You're not upset, are you?"

"Actually I think they know me better than I know myself. This has been wonderful. I'd highly recommend surprise weddings."

Dillon's laughter drew everyone's attention to them. "She recommends surprise weddings," he explained.

The laughter echoed throughout the group.

The reception was just as stunning. Snowy white cloths draped tables filled with white china and silver. The food was tremendous, and each setting had its own miniature version of the beautiful wedding cake.

"You must have spent hours doing all these cakes," Maggie declared as she and Dillon sliced into the cake for the photographer. The bride and groom atop the cake looked like a caricature of the two of them.

"You're worth it," Natalie said, turning to speak to a woman who asked about a cake.

Avery walked over.

"You did a fantastic job," Maggie told him.

"Glad you like it. I know I've been wrong for the way I've treated Natalie. I apologized to her."

"Sometimes we can't see beyond ourselves," Maggie told him. "The important thing is to be friends in Christ. In the end, that's all that matters."

"Did Avery tell you we're planning to enter a version of your cake in a contest?" Natalie asked after she finished her conversation and turned back to them.

"Wow. You two really have come a long way."

"All thanks to you and Dillon," Natalie pointed out. "If not for this surprise wedding, we'd probably still be at odds with each other."

"God works in mysterious ways," Dillon said.

"That He does," Maggie agreed, slipping her arm about Dillon's waist. "I love you, Mr. Rogers."

"And I love you, my incredible Maggie Rogers. You've made coming home the best thing I ever did." He kissed her, and Natalie and Avery playfully cleared their throats.

Joe came over to offer his congratulations.

"I hope you didn't mind rescheduling," he said.

"We didn't mind at all," Dillon said. "I'm sorry Chester Simpson ended up at the hospital though."

"He didn't stay," Maggie said. "He gave me a thumbs-up when I walked down the aisle."

"And you're not upset over all the secrecy?" Joe asked.

"Not at all."

Joe clapped Dillon on the shoulder. "I think he lost sleep over keeping it from you."

"But I'm glad he did," Maggie announced. "The memories of this special day will stay with us forever. Having so much love focused on us helped me realize that in Jesus we will never be foster children. We're the real thing, and we always have a home with our heavenly Father."

All three sets of eyes grew misty with her revelation.

"Welcome home, darling," Dillon declared as he wrapped his arms about her.

"Amen," Joe Dennis declared.

epilogue

Two years later

"Still tired?" Dillon asked as they walked toward the church.

Maggie nodded. They had arrived home from a month-long Australian tour just two days before. Though tired, she knew she'd never forget the experience. "It'll take time to get over the jet lag."

"By next week I hope," Dillon said. "We're getting a foster child placement on Monday."

Maggie smiled. Over the past two years, Maggie Rogers had seen more of the world than she'd ever imagined. She'd given up her job and concentrated on being a good wife. They'd honeymooned in Paris and then gone to Saudi Arabia so Dillon could introduce her to his friends. They'd taken an Alaskan cruise and frequently traveled in the United States. She'd even accompanied him on a couple of mission trips.

"Oh, I almost forgot," she said, drawing the strand of pearls from his coat pocket.

Dillon leaned to kiss her after he secured the necklace in place. "I love you, Maggie. Not a day goes by that I don't thank God for bringing us together."

She turned in his arms. "I love you more every day, too, Dillon. Having you as my husband has made me so happy." The sounds of slamming car doors and people's laughter intruded on their moment. "We'd better hurry, or we'll be late." Inside the church, Maggie touched his cheek and said, "See you down front."

He paused a second longer and winked at her.

She smiled and opened the door to the bride's room.

"There you are," the women called in unison.

Maggie's gaze moved from friend to friend. Each one so precious—her sisters in Christ—the family she'd longed for.

She was proud to call Mari Dennis her friend and Joe Dennis her pastor. The Dennis children were growing up so fast; and Luke had become even more attached to Mr. Dillon. Maggie knew Dillon felt the same about him.

Julie, Noah, and little Joshua had arrived the day before. Noah had been called to a church in Tennessee, and they all missed Julie a great deal. They remained in touch and were delighted that she'd grown to love being a pastor's wife.

Maggie walked over and hugged her. "Where's Josh?"

"With Diana. She's keeping him and Sarah today."

Kim's mother was truly in her element with the little girl who had stolen all their hearts.

"She said to tell you she's sorry she can't be here, Natalie," Kim said as she pinned the veil in place. "Though I'm pretty sure you'd prefer not to have them carrying on during your ceremony. Mom has Sarah spoiled rotten."

Maggie walked over and hugged Kim. "I don't think your mom is the only culprit."

Kim grinned and said, "Welcome home."

"Thanks. How are you feeling today?" Maggie asked, noting Kim's expanded waistline and thinking it wouldn't be long before little Sarah had a brother or sister.

"Okay. Mom's taken a lot of the load off by helping with Sarah and the store."

"Are we still on for tonight?" Julie asked. "I told Noah we're having girls' night. Sure you don't want to stick around, Nat?"

Natalie shook her head and said, "Not this time."

Peg called hello, and Maggie decided she looked much happier. Peg's estranged husband had been killed in a bar fight the year before. Six months later, Maggie and Peg had gone out to lunch and encountered William Smith. Maggie introduced them, and he had asked Peg out. All the Smith men adored Peg and Chloe, and Maggie saw a wedding in her friend's future.

Maggie walked over to help Peg sort the flowers. "Where's Chloe?"

"Will and the boys are keeping an eye on her."

Maggie smiled and said, "Hey, Nat, you need to aim that bouquet in Peg's direction today."

"That's my plan," their friend declared.

Kim grinned at Maggie and said, "You should give her some advice on the best way to catch one."

Maggie laughed at her teasing. "Just jump right out in front and accept the inevitable. It makes things easier all around."

"Well, what do you think?" Natalie asked as she twirled about in her wedding dress.

"You look like you belong on top of a cake," Maggie teased, hugging her friend.

Maggie and Dillon's wedding had brought Natalie and Avery together in Christian fellowship, and they had become quite a team. Recently, she and Dillon had watched when they won the grand prize at a wedding cake competition on television.

"You make a beautiful bride."

"Who would have thought it?" Natalie asked.

"Jesus," Maggie supplied. "The very Cornerstone of our existence."

The music started and Natalie said, "Can we pray?"

They all bowed their heads, each thanking God for this precious family He'd given them.

A Letter To Our Readers

Dear Reader:
In order that we might better contribute to your reading enjoyment, we would appreciate your taking a few minutes to respond to the following questions. We welcome your comments and read each form and letter we receive. When completed, please return to the following:

Fiction Editor
Heartsong Presents
PO Box 719
Uhrichsville, Ohio 44683

1. Did you enjoy reading *Coming Home* by Terry Fowler?
   ❑ Very much! I would like to see more books by this author!
   ❑ Moderately. I would have enjoyed it more if

   _____
   _____
   _____

2. Are you a member of **Heartsong Presents**? ❑ Yes ❑ No
   If no, where did you purchase this book? _____
   _____

3. How would you rate, on a scale from 1 (poor) to 5 (superior), the cover design? _____

4. On a scale from 1 (poor) to 10 (superior), please rate the following elements.

   ____ Heroine   ____ Plot
   ____ Hero   ____ Inspirational theme
   ____ Setting   ____ Secondary characters

5. These characters were special because? _____

_____

_____

6. How has this book inspired your life? _____

_____

_____

7. What settings would you like to see covered in future
   Heartsong Presents books? _____

_____

_____

8. What are some inspirational themes you would like to see
   treated in future books? _____

_____

_____

9. Would you be interested in reading other **Heartsong
   Presents** titles? ❑ Yes   ❑ No

10. Please check your age range:
       ❑ Under 18   ❑ 18-24
       ❑ 25-34   ❑ 35-45
       ❑ 46-55   ❑ Over 55

Name _____

Occupation _____

Address _____

City, State, Zip_____

Heartsong

HEARTSONG PRESENTS TITLES AVAILABLE NOW:

Presents

Great Inspirational Romance at a Great Price!

Heartsong Presents books are inspirational romances in
contemporary and historical settings, designed to give you an
enjoyable, spirit-lifting reading experience. You can choose
wonderfully written titles from some of today's best authors like
Wanda E. Brunstetter, Mary Connealy, Susan Page Davis,
Cathy Marie Hake, Joyce Livingston, and many others.

When ordering quantities less than twelve, above titles are $2.97 each.
Not all titles may be available at time of order.